A Touch of

Magical Midlife: the K

By

Rose Bak

Table of Contents

Copyright 1

About This Book 2

Join My Mailing List 3

Love Potion 4

Copyright 5

About This Book 6

Prologue—Cami 7

Cami 10

Stephen 15

Cami 19

Stephen 27

Cami 31

Stephen 37

Cami 42

Stephen 48

Cami 53

Stephen 57

Epilogue—Cami 63

Psychic Flashes 65

Copyright 66

About This Book 67

Dedication 68

Meri 69

Preston 72

Meri 76

Preston 80

Meri 83

Preston 87

Meri 91

Preston 95

Meri 98

Preston 103

Meri 108

Preston 112

Meri 117

Preston 122

Meri 127

Epilogue - Preston 133

Kitchen Magic 136

Copyright 137

About This Book 138

Dedication 139

Prologue—Pepper 140

Pepper 142

Charles 145

Pepper 149

Charles 153

Pepper 157

Charles 161

Pepper 165

Charles 169

Pepper 174

Charles 178

Pepper 182

Charles 186

Pepper 191

Charles 195

Pepper 199

Charles 205

Epilogue – Pepper 210

Special Preview 213

Other Books by Rose Bak 217

About the Author 220

Copyright

About This Book

3 magical sisters. 3 funny paranormal love stories.

Just outside the shifter town of Greysden sits Rosewater Manor, a place shrouded in magic. The Rosewater sisters all have special gifts, although sometimes they're a bit glitchy. At least until they find true love...

This three book midlife romance collection includes:

- *Love Potion*
- *Psychic Flashes*
- *Kitchen Magic*

About the "Magical Midlife" series: Just outside the shifter town of Greysden sits Rosewater Manor, a place shrouded in magic. The Rosewater women and their friends all have special gifts, although sometimes they're a bit glitchy. At least until they find true love...

Check out these instalove romantic comedies if you enjoy fated mates who start off as rejected mates, midlife characters, eccentric small towns, nosy friends and family intent on matchmaking, steamy scenes, and sweet happily ever afters.

Join My Mailing List

Join Rose Bak's mailing list at bit.ly/RoseBakNewsletter[1]. You'll get a free book and be the first to hear about all the latest releases and special sales.

1. https://d.docs.live.net/ae511949052ccd53/Documents/bit.ly/RoseBakNewsletter

Love Potion

Magical Midlife
Rose Bak

Copyright

About This Book

The love spell worked...on the wrong sister!

When her sister begs her to do a love spell to attract her true mate, Cami is hesitant. Her magic is glitchy on a good day. But what's the harm of trying? To everyone's shock, the spell manifests exactly the man they hoped for, except for one problem...he's in love with Cami, not her sister.

Shapeshifter Stephen doesn't believe in magic, but he does believe in fate. His wolf knows the truth: Cami is his true mate, the one he's destined to be together with forever. If only Cami could forget about the spell and listen to her heart...

"Love Potion" is a steamy standalone featuring a midlife couple, matchmaking sisters, and a little touch of magic leading to a happy ending.

Prologue—Cami

"Come on, Cami! You're the only one who can help me."

"Pepper, you know what Mom always said. We shouldn't mess around with magic unless we really know what we're doing."

"You're a witch. You do know what you're doing."

I shook my head as I looked at my younger sister. I couldn't decide if she really had that much faith in my abilities, such as they were, or if she was just blowing smoke up my you-know-what to get me to give her what she wanted. Maybe a bit of both.

My two sisters and I were the product of a mixed marriage. Mom was a witch and Dad was human, but not a normal, he was also a psychic. The pairing had affected all of us differently. I had some magical tendences, although they tended to glitch a lot. Our youngest sister Meri was psychic. At least kind of psychic. Most of her visons were pretty useless to be honest. She could predict that you'd break your phone screen tomorrow, but she couldn't predict the lottery numbers or anything that was actually helpful. And Pepper, our middle sister, didn't seem to have any powers. At least none that we'd discovered so far.

"You know the first rule of witchcraft Pepper. Do no harm." Our mother had drilled that into us over and over when we were growing up.

"How would opening the path for my true love to find me do harm?" Pepper cocked her head to the side and gave me the entreating look she'd perfected way back when we were kids. "I'm thirty-four years old, I want to find my true love before my eggs shrivel up and I can't have kids anymore. The clock is ticking here."

I sighed. She'd been bugging me about this for weeks and I was tired of arguing with her.

"Fine, I'll do a spell." I held up a finger as my sister squealed with delight. "But I'll only do a spell to clear the path for you to find your true love, if the universe has one identified for you. But you need to be prepared that if there's no one destined to be with you, or the time isn't right for you to find your mate, the spell won't work."

"Fine, I get it, Chamomile. Whatever. Just hook me up and I'll take care of the rest."

I shot her a glare at her use of my full name. Our mom was...eccentric. As a witch, she used a lot of herbs and medicinal plants. For some reason that made her think it would be a good idea to name us all after plants. As if our lives weren't weird enough already.

"Kiss my ass, Peppermint."

Pepper rolled her eyes. "When can you do it?"

"The new moon is in a couple of days. I'll look up what we need and then we can do it by the river. We'll get Meri to help."

"Turmeric is a fuddy duddy. She never wants to do spells." Our youngest sister Meri was the least spiritual of all of us.

"She'll help, don't worry."

A few days later we three sisters gathered on the bank of the river that ran through the back of our family's land. The Rosewaters had lived on this land for over a hundred years, and each generation passed the land onto the next. Our mother and her sister had grown up here, and while Aunt Pat had moved away from the craziness of our magical world, Mom had raised us here. She and Dad were retired now and traveling the world, so we had the place to ourselves.

Some people thought it was weird for three grown women in their thirties to live together in their family home, but we weren't crazy. Rosewater Manor was huge, and we all had our own suites. Best of all, we owned it outright so there was no mortgage to pay. The house was well-equipped and came with household staff who did most of the cooking and cleaning, paid for by the large trust fund my mom had inherited from her parents. There was no way any of us would trade in a crappy one-bedroom apartment for the easy luxury of the Manor. Not unless we had a reason to, anyway.

The night was dark and clear as my sisters and I walked through the woods on our property and headed for the river. We found a flat space on the ground to set up. Using our flashlights to help us see, we quickly created a circle made from river stones, and the three of us settled inside the circle. Pepper and Meri built a small fire in the center of the circle while I gathered the other supplies for the spell, stopping a couple of times to refer to the notes on my phone. I didn't want to mess things up and summon my sister a demon instead of a husband.

"OK, we're ready."

We held hands and closed our eyes, slowing our breaths just as our mother had taught us. I began to draw forth the powers of my magic.

"Pepper, tell the universe what you'd like in a mate."

"He should be tall, dark, and handsome. Broad like a football player."

"Bring a mate who is tall," I intoned. "Bring a mate with hair like a raven. Bring a mate who is strong of body and handsome to the eye."

"Oh, and I want someone who's an animal in the sheets."

I rolled my eyes, not that Pepper could see it when we all had our eyes closed, and dutifully added, "Bring a mate who has animal tendencies."

I threw the magical herbs into the fire as I chanted the spell incantation. Turning my inner gaze up to my third eye – the space between my eyebrows—I tried to visualize the man my sister wanted to find. In my mind's eye I conjured a tall, broad man with wide shoulders and strong legs. I imagined dark hair and dark eyes, a man who was both wild and kind. I pressed my hands into the Earth and felt the light hum of magic thrumming though my fingertips.

"So shall it be."

Cami

A few days had passed since we'd done the spell in the woods. Pepper had been insufferable since then. During the day she roamed around town, hoping to run into her future husband, and at night she badgered me non-stop about if I thought the spell would work and how long it would take for someone to find her. It was as if she thought there was some kind of "thirty days or your money back" guarantee on magic.

On the third day I invited Pepper and Meri to go for a hike to take everyone's mind off the spell. Summer was coming and it was a warm, sunny day. Our family property backed up onto the woods, making it a perfect access point to a variety of trails through the forest. It was a warm, sunny day and the woods were alive with the smells and sounds of Spring. We'd been hiking for about half an hour when Meri suddenly stopped and clutched her head, a sure sign she was having one of her psychic visions.

"The wolf. It slips its collar."

Pepper and I looked at each other, then back at our sister. That was weird, even for Meri.

"What did you see?" Pepper asked her curiously.

Meri shook her head, then froze, her eyes wide. Shakily she raised one hand and pointed behind us. "That."

I turned around to look in the direction Meri was pointed, and gasped as I saw a wolf stalking towards us. It was the largest wolf I'd ever seen, but its eyes looked human. Oh thank the Goddess, it was just a wolf shifter not a real wild wolf. We knew shifters wouldn't hurt us. Our little town seemed to attract all manner of magical creatures, including shape shifters.

"What's up, Wolfie?" I asked as the wolf stopped in front of me, staring up at me intently.

The air around us shimmered. Cracking and popping noises filled the air and in an instant, the wolf in front of me changed into a man. A naked man. A hot as hell naked man.

"Mate!" he growled, his deep voice still more wolf than human as he stared at me. "I found you!"

Praise to the Goddess, he was a fine specimen. He was tall and dark and built like a line backer. His dark eyes burned like coals against his tan face. A light scruff covered his square jaw and, oh crap, my kryptonite—he had a chin cleft. Yum. And he clearly had an animal side. But why was he here?

Oh! This suddenly made sense. He was just as I'd visualized when I'd done the love spell for my sister. A sense of loss rolled through me as I shook my head and pointed at Pepper.

"You're here for her, Wolfie, not me."

Pepper stepped forward, her eyes wide as she examined the wide shoulders, the hard planes of his chest, the muscled arms, and the happy trail that ran from the bottom of his eight pack abs to an erect cock that was, well, let's just say it was proportionate to the rest of him.

I tamped down the sudden jealous urge to push Pepper out of the way and block him from my sister's eager eyes. After all, she was the one who'd called for him. This man was going to be my brother-in-law. I couldn't be lusting after him, that was just gross. I stifled a sigh. Pepper had all the luck.

"It's me," Pepper confirmed, giving him a little wave. "I'm your mate. You're here for me."

The man shook his head, sparing Pepper a quick glance before his intense gaze returned to me. My entire body tingled as he looked me up and down, his gaze almost like a touch.

"Mate, I've been looking for you my whole life."

I could see the truth in his eyes. This man, this shifter, he truly believed I was his mate. I tried not to notice how warm and fuzzy that made me feel. My whole life, no one had ever chosen me. Pepper was the pretty sister, and Meri was the life of the party. Me? I was the smart nerdy sister, the quiet one who guys were mostly nice to in order to meet one of my sisters.

He's not for you, I reminded myself. *You have to fix this.*

The wolf sniffed. "You're not a shifter, mate, but I sense magic in you. Are you a fae?"

"She's a witch," Meri piped up. Her amused gaze switched between me and the stranger. "Maybe not the best one though."

Pepper finally caught up. "Wait a minute," she poked the guy in the biceps, trying to get his attention again. "You really think Chamomile here is your mate?"

The man straightened as he turned to face my sister.

"I know she is my mate, without a doubt. I live over in Greysden, about thirty minutes from here. My wolf was restless, wanting to go for a run, and directed me here. As soon as he smelled his mate," he turned his head to give me another searing gaze before directing his attention back to Pepper. "As soon as we picked up her sweet scent, I lost control of my wolf and he brought me here. To her. She is my fated mate, the other half of my soul. My wolf knows."

Pepper threw up her hands in aggravation. "Damn it, Cami, I thought you knew how to at least do a simple spell without messing it up!"

"What spell?" the stranger asked.

"Cami did a love spell that was supposed to help me find my true love." She dragged out the word 'supposed' with a sarcastic tone. "You look like just what I asked for. But she must have fucked it up somehow, because you're focused on the wrong sister."

"She isn't the wrong sister," he corrected, his voice deep and sure. "This one is my mate. Chamomile." He tried out my name like it was foreign to him, then reached out one large hand. "I'm Stephen."

Our palms touched and I gasped as a jolt of electricity ran through my body. I had the sudden urge to climb him like a tree. Stephen's nostrils flared, telling me he could smell the rush of arousal that had dampened my panties the minute we touched. Damn shifters.

"Nice to meet you, Stephen. My friends call me Cami." My voice sounded breathy, and I cringed internally. This was just the spell. I had to remember that. I wasn't this guy's soulmate, as much as I might wish it were true. Goddess, I wished it were true. "I'm sorry, but I'm not your mate. There's been a terrible mistake."

"I'll figure out how to reverse it," I told Pepper. "I just need to figure out what went wrong with the magic, then I can fix it. I promise."

She looked disgusted. "Never mind. The dude's fixated on you now. I'm not going to be his sloppy seconds."

Pepper's voice turned sad. "It figures that this would happen to me. I guess I'll never find love. I might as well embrace my old maid status. I'm going to dye my hair grey, stop wearing underwire bras, and go buy a bunch of cats."

"But you hate cats," I protested. She was also a little too busty to eschew underwires, but I didn't want to add insult to injury.

She grabbed Meri's hand and gave her a tug, pulling her away from me and the shifter. "Come on, let's give these kids some privacy."

"Pepper..." I called after my sister, but she and Meri were already gone. Both of them could move fast when they wanted to. I sighed deeply. Damn it. I felt terrible about upsetting my sister.

"What's the matter, mate?" Stephen asked. "Are you disappointed in me for some reason?"

I looked at him, my eyes traveling from his big feet, which were somehow attractive even though I hated feet, up his muscled body, and over the handsome lines of his face. He was hot as hell, but I knew what I was feeling was just because of the spell. I'd never been attracted to a guy like this before. My type was more like blonde and lean, not dark and broad, but even still, I somehow knew deep in my soul that he was perfect for me. Except for the pesky issue of him being my sister's mate.

I patted his bare chest with my hand, then regretted it immediately as the touch of our skin made another wave of arousal flow through me so strongly my knees almost buckled.

"It's not that I'm disappointed," I reassured him. I didn't know this guy, but I still didn't want to hurt his feelings.

"I'm sure you're a great guy. And you're not hard on the eyes, that's for sure. But you're here because of a spell. I messed it up somehow; I actually summoned you here for my sister, Pepper."

He nodded. "Yeah, I got that, but you're wrong," he said with a touch of arrogance in his tone that annoyed me. "I'm a shifter, our mates are determined by the fates themselves, not some witch's silly spell. You're the one I'm supposed to be with. My finding you after you did a spell for your sister is just a coincidence."

"Magic isn't silly," I protested. "You look exactly like what my sister said she wanted."

"Do you really think the way we feel right now is only because of your magic?" he asked, stepping closer. "Do you think I can't smell that you're as attracted to me as I am to you, little mate?"

Alpha energy was coming off this guy in waves. I took a step back, suddenly nervous. He followed, eyes darkening as he stalked me like prey. I took another step, then another, until my back hit a tree. Stephen crowded up close to me, putting one hand on either side of my head, his large palms pressing into the bark. He was as close as he could be without actually touching me. The air around us was thick and felt charged. My body was vibrating with awareness, and it took every bit of my self-control to not close the distance between us.

"If it's not magic, I don't know what this is," I whispered.

"It's fate."

Stephen

The minute my lips touched Cami's I knew my wolf had been right. Cami was my fated mate. The one being in all the world who was meant just for me. Not that I doubted him, not really, but any hesitation my human side felt faded away as I kissed her.

Every cell in my body stilled and a sense of peace filled me. I'd heard my parents talk about this, the sense of rightness that a shifter felt the first time they kissed their mate. I'd disregarded their stories as romantic fantasies, but this was no fantasy. It was a dream come true.

I nipped at her bottom lip, demanding entrance into the sweet heat of her mouth. She complied, sighing as my tongue swept in and tangled with hers.

My mate was perfect. Better than I could have ever hoped for. She was on the tall side, maybe five eight to my six foot two height. She had long straight brown hair that went past her shoulders, and large brown eyes that stood in contrast to the paleness of her white face. Her features were sharp, except her mouth which looked like the cutest little red bow. She was curvy as hell, with large pendulous breast, thick thighs, and a slim waist that gently sloped into full hips. Fate had chosen well. I couldn't have described a more attractive mate even if I'd done a spell of my own.

I chuckled internally, thinking of her insistence that the attraction between us was due to some spell. I'd grown up around witches – this entire part of the state was full of magical beings, attracted by the energy vortexes that converged under the Earth in this area. One thing I knew about spells: there was always an element of choice. A person could resist a witch's spell if they were strong willed enough, but no one could resist the shifter mating call. Shifters would die rather than be away from their true mates.

She's ours, my wolf confirmed. *We must mark her and stake our claim.*

15

I could feel my canines pushing at my gums, my wolf eager to sink its teeth into the softness of Cami's milky white neck. But I knew instinctively that it would be a mistake to rush her. I pulled back from the kiss and stared down into my mate's beautiful face. Her eyes were glassy, and she looked a little dazed. I felt a sense of pride that I'd affected her like that. She wasn't the only one who felt off-kilter.

"I want nothing more than to take you against this tree and make you mine," I started. My cock twitched as the sweet scent of her increased arousal hit my nostrils. "But I think you need time to adjust to the news of us finding each other."

Cami straightened, her eyes clearing as the haze of attraction ebbed. "Look Wolfie, I don't want a mate, and even if I did, I can't do this to my sister. I won't hurt her like this. Sisters before Misters, that's been our sacred vow since we grew breasts."

She placed a hand on my chest, her palm searing me like a brand. I let her push me away, even as my wolf whined deep inside me. *Be patient,* I chastised him. He wasn't the most patient animal.

"I'm sorry, but I've got to get home and figure out how to fix this spell."

"Do you really want me to be with your sister?" I asked curiously. "You want me to kiss her the way I just kissed you?"

Her eyes blazed with anger before she tamped it down again. Her reaction gave me comfort.

"You don't understand. She put an intention out to the universe, asking for her perfect man. She described you in great detail and you're just as she described. The perfect man for her."

"I'm the perfect man for you Cami." Her eyes flew to mine as I pressed on. "And you're the perfect woman for me. Not your sister. You."

"You don't even know me," she argued. "It's best if we just say goodbye."

"I don't need to know you. My wolf knows you. And we're not going to give you up without a fight Cami. I need you. And I think you need me too."

She was shaking her head before I even finished. "No. This can't happen. I need to go."

"Play with your potions as much as you want, little witch. That won't change anything. I've got fate on my side."

I stalked over and kissed her softly on the forehead. "I'll come see you tomorrow."

"You mean you'll come see Pepper."

I shook my head. "I said exactly what I mean. Until tomorrow, mate."

"You don't even know where I live," she said confidently.

I tapped the side of my nose. "I don't need to know, my wolf will sniff you out."

She rolled her eyes. "Damn shifters."

With one last look at my mate, I stepped back and inhaled deeply, calling my wolf forward. The air around me shifted and I felt the familiar sensation of my bones breaking and lengthening, muscles expanding, claws and fangs extending. Dark fur pushed through my pores, and I dropped to all fours.

When the change was complete, I padded over to my mate, who stood watching nearby. I nudged her with my head, and she leaned down to stroke the fur between my ears. My wolf preened happily.

"Bye Wolfie," she whispered sadly.

I held my wolf back as she hurried away, assuring him that we would find her again tomorrow. Maybe by then she'd have had enough time to accept our pairing. Connecting with a fated mate was always easier when both parties were shifters, but I was confident she would come around.

I ambled back through the woods, heading to where I'd parked my car. The ground was soft underneath my paws due a recent rainstorm, and my wolf inhaled the fresh damp air as I continued on my journey. I loved this part of being a shifter. Being one with the forest, hearing the animals skittering around as they sensed my approach, smelling all the scents of growth and decay that I couldn't detect when I was in my human form. It felt so freeing to run like this. But no run had ever been so joyous.

I'd finally found my mate. I had turned forty a few months ago, and after so many years alone I had started to worry that I'd never have a mate. My siblings had settled down with their mates, embarking on long happy marriages just like our parents had. Mom and Dad had been mates for fifty years and married for nearly as long. We were planning their fiftieth anniversary party later this year, and I couldn't wait to celebrate with my mate by my side.

I just needed to get her off this idea that her spell had gone wrong and that I was intended for her sister. Either her spell hadn't worked, or it had worked but the sister's mate hadn't found her yet. Either way, it was an unfortunate coincidence that I'd found her right after she'd tried to help her sister. I wasn't going to let that stop me though. I wanted to spend the rest of my life with my mate, and I was eager for the rest of my life to start right away.

Besides, if Pepper was a decent woman, she would want her sister to be happy. And she wouldn't want me to be with her when she knew my heart belonged to Cami.

I'd find Cami tomorrow and talk some sense into her. If all else failed, I could just throw her over my shoulder, bring her back to my den, and kiss her until she realized the truth. Cami was mine.

Cami

As soon as I got back to the Rosewater Mansion, I started looking for Pepper. I found her in the library, thumbing through an old photo album with a sad expression on her face. She looked like she'd lost her best friend – or her mate. My heart pinched at her sadness.

"Hey," I said, coming to sit in the chair across from her. "I'm so so sorry Pepper. I don't know what happened. I swear I was only focused on you during the spell. You know that I don't even want a mate."

"No, but your mate wants you," she said sadly. "I'm not mad at you Cami, if that's what you're worried about. I know you did your best, and I want you to be happy as much as I want that for myself. If that wolf makes you happy, then so be it. I wish you both the best, truly."

I shook my head. "No, I'm going to figure out how to reverse the spell and we can do it again."

"No, that's not necessary. I was talking to Meri, and she said something that made a lot of sense. A love spell is too personal to put in someone else's hands, even if that someone else is as close as we are. That's what went wrong with the spell. I should have done it myself, if only I had some power."

It was a source of ongoing frustration for Pepper that I'd inherited some of Mom's magic, and Meri had some of Dad's psychic abilities, glitchy as they both were, but Pepper was just a regular human with no supernatural talent at all. Or if she had some, it had never manifested.

I sighed deeply. "I wish Mom was here, she would have known how to do the spell properly."

A flush rose up Pepper's face. "Um. Well, the thing is, I asked Mom first."

"What?"

"I asked her last time she was in town to do a love spell for me, and she refused. She said it was a terrible idea. She said that I couldn't rush

19

fate and that the universe would bring me someone in good time if I was just patient and made myself open to the possibilities."

I felt a wave of irritation. "Mom said it was a bad idea, so you asked me? Even knowing that my powers are sporadic and quirky?"

She nodded. "Yeah, I figured it was either try it with you or visit a sperm bank. I guess I'll be visiting a sperm bank."

"Peppermint Mugwort Rosewater, you are NOT going to a sperm bank!"

My sister grimaced at my use of her full name. None of us sisters were particularly fond of our weird names.

"I can if I want to, Chamomile Ginseng Rosewater, you're not the boss of me."

I rolled my eyes at her childish retort. "How do you think your soulmate will feel when he finds you and you're walking around with some anonymous guy's kid?"

"I really don't care how some imaginary guy that I may or may not ever meet would feel. This is about me. It's my life, and I've wanted to be a mother since I was five years old. I'm sick of waiting to have a family. You were my last hope."

I moved towards her and leaned down to give her a hug. "You can be your own hope, Pepper. Someone is out there for you, someone perfect, and you'll find each other soon. I just know it."

Pepper hugged me back. "Thanks Sis, I hope you're right. So, what are you going to do about your new mate?"

"Nothing." I felt a stab of pain behind my sternum as I spoke. "I'm not going to see him again. I told him it was all a mistake, and that I didn't want a mate, not now, not ever."

"How did that go?" she asked, her voice amused.

I kneeled on the floor in front of her chair and met her gaze. "He kissed me."

I could feel redness climbing up my neck and cursed my fair complexion. Kissed seemed like an understatement. It was more like a claiming. He'd ravished me with his mouth, and I'd loved every minute of it. But there was no way I was going into that with my sister. I could hardly admit it to myself.

"How was it?"

"Really good," I admitted sheepishly. "He's hot as hell, obviously, but I'd never do anything to hurt you, Pepper. You're my sister, and that's way more important than any boy."

"That boy is all man. My Goddess, did you see his giant..."

She broke off laughing as I smacked her arm. "Hey!"

Pepper leaned forward and grasped my face between her palms. "I want you to be happy as much as you want the same for me, Chamomile. You should go for it with your wolf. You have my blessing."

I shook my head. "I'm not even sure if I'll see him again, besides, you know I like being single."

"You don't know a lot about shifter mates, do you? There's no way that guy is going to stay away if you're really his mate. You'd better buckle up big sister, because I think you're in for the ride of your life."

I spent a restless night thinking about Stephen and wondering if I really was going to see him again. I hadn't been lying; I didn't want a mate. Sure, I enjoyed sex as much as the next girl, but having the same guy around day in and day out? Relying on someone else for your happiness? There was no way that I wanted that for myself. My parents were happily married, but I'd never really wanted that life, especially after my bad experience with an ex-boyfriend. I was content to be the cool weird aunt for Meri and Pepper's kids. Or I would be if either of them ever fell in love and had a family. I just wished I knew what I'd done wrong with that spell to make it backfire.

The next day the wooing started. I woke up to flowers being delivered to my house. A ridiculously large arrangement with a sweet card saying, *Beautiful flowers for my beautiful mate. Can I take you to dinner tonight?* The card included his phone number. I threw it in the trash but kept the flowers. I wasn't a total monster.

Meri texted me later that day. I was at work when Stephen showed up at the house at dinner time asking to see me. He tried to charm her out of my phone number, but my baby sister held firm. The following day more flowers came, followed by a life-sized stuffed wolf with a bow around its neck, and a few hours later, a giant box of candy. Each gift came with an entreaty to call him, which I ignored. Maybe he'd get the message that I wasn't interested. Meanwhile my sisters were pressing me to give him a chance, much to my annoyance.

On the third day I was working at the store as usual. Early on in their marriage, my parents had opened a combination bookstore, magic shop, and café called Rosewater's Magical Emporium. We'd all worked there growing up, but neither Pepper nor Meri really loved it the way I did. They helped out when needed, but they didn't have any interest in working there on a daily basis. Not like me. Rosewater's was my life.

I had studied business administration in college and after graduation I'd dedicated myself to learning all aspects of the business from Mom and Dad, working my way up from stocking shelves to being the store manager. I'd saved my money and was able to buy them out when they'd finally retired last year. Under my leadership the last thirteen years, the shop had grown and expanded into a neighboring shop, developed a social media following, and created an online store that now had better sales than our bricks and mortar store. I was proud of all my accomplishments.

The bell rang over the door just after five o'clock, and I stuck my head out in the aisle from where I was stocking shelves. I'd sent my staff person on their dinner break, so I was the only person working in the store right now besides the high school girl who was working in the back of the store at the café.

"Welcome to Rosewater's. How may I..."

I froze as a hulking figure came around a display, and my stomach dropped. It was Stephen, looking yummy as hell in faded jeans that lovingly hugged his muscular thighs, and a plain grey t-shirt that stretched tight against his enormous biceps. My mouth was immediately dry.

"Mate." His growl seemed to carry across the store as his eyes raked over me, taking in my long black knit skirt, dark pink scoop neck t-shirt, and beaded jewelry. My nipples immediately hardened, and his eyes dropped, telling me that my reaction was visible beneath the thin fabric of my shirt and bra.

"Um. Hi. How may I help you?" I asked. "We're having a sale on cozy mysteries if you're interested."

"Do you work here?" he asked, noting the opened box of books at my feet.

I nodded. "I own this shop," I told him with pride in my voice. "This section is books, and that side is for metaphysical items like crystals, tarot cards, and magical supplies. There's also a café in the back if you'd like a coffee while you shop."

"I didn't come here to shop," he told me. "I came to see my mate."

I ignored the thrill I felt at his words. "How did you find me?"

He pressed one finger against the side of his nose like he had done the other day. Damn, he wasn't kidding about being able to track me by scent. It was a little weird to think that was possible. It's not like I didn't shower. I leaned into my irritation and stepped closer, close enough that I could see his eyes glowing with his wolf.

"Maybe I wasn't clear the other day, but I summoned you by accident. It's my sister who's looking for a mate, not me. I'm not interested." I pointed in the direction of the door. "You should go now."

"Maybe I wasn't clear," he said, repeating my words. "I am not under the influence of some spell. You are my mate. Only you. My arrival after you did your little spell was just a coincidence."

He stepped closer and I stepped back, waving my hand at him, and muttering a magic incantation. A puff of smoke rose between us, then disappeared into vapor. Damn my glitchy magic. I meant to put up a force field between us to keep him away.

He raised one dark eyebrow. "That the best you can do?"

"I never said I was good at being a witch," I replied defensively.

He reached a hand out and cupped my cheek. Instinctively I leaned into his touch. It felt so...right. "I'd like to spend some time with you, Mate, so we can get to know each other better before I claim you."

"I don't think that's a good idea," I protested, even though I didn't sound particularly convincing. I hoped he couldn't smell the rush of arousal that flooded my core at his words.

"What time do you get off work?" he asked. I tried to be annoyed that he was ignoring me, but somehow, I couldn't. A small part of me appreciated his single-minded focus on me, even though I would never admit that.

"I'm working until closing time," I responded. "Maybe I'll see you some other time."

"I'll just grab a cup of coffee and wait until you're done then."

"But..."

"You said the café is back here?" he said, walking backwards and pointing in the direction of the café.

"But..."

"Just let me know when you're ready to go."

"But..."

He disappeared around the corner of the shelves as I stared after him with my mouth open.

"You might as well give up. You summoned a stubborn one." I jumped as I heard Meri's amused voice behind me.

"Meri! I didn't hear you come in!"

My youngest sister laughed. "Yeah, you didn't even twitch when the bell over the door rang. You were a little busy with your new boyfriend."

I stared at her. Over the years I'd become so conditioned to hear that bell over the door that I was like one of Pavlov's dogs. I heard the bell when I was back in my office. I heard the bell in the alley when I was taking out the trash. I even heard it in my sleep. I never missed the bell. I couldn't believe that damn wolf had distracted me so much.

Meri put her hands on her hips. "So what's your beef with the big guy?" she asked, nodding in the direction that Stephen had gone. I'd ignored that same question from her for the last two days, but this time I answered.

"First of all, I did a spell to find the perfect mate for Pepper, not for myself."

"Pepper doesn't care about that, and I know she's told you that. It was a stupid idea anyway, both of you should have known it wasn't going to work."

"Second," I continued as if she hadn't spoken. "I don't want a mate."

"Yeah, I could see why you wouldn't want a big hulky guy who fate ordained is perfect for you," she said, her voice laden with sarcasm. "Why would you want someone who will be physically incapable of abandoning you or cheating on you. Someone who will protect you and never hurt you. I mean, my Goddess, who would want that?"

"Third," I pressed on. "I like my life the way it is right now. I have no time for a boyfriend, let alone a mate."

My sister rolled her eyes. "Well, I don't know why fate is wasting a perfectly good mate on someone like you, Chamomile. I mean sure, both Pepper and I would die to have someone to love us, but instead the perfect man goes to the one sister who won't appreciate it."

"Are you done being dramatic?" I asked.

She nodded.

"Can you finish my shift for me?" I asked. "I can tell this guy's not going to leave me alone until I go out with him and talk some sense into him." Ignoring him wasn't helping, so I figured I'd go grab a drink with him or something so he could see for himself what a terrible match we were.

"Sure Sis, I'll finish your shift for you, don't worry. You go hang out with your looove." Meri drew out the last work teasingly.

Before I could snap back a retort there was a blur and a rush of air, and then Stephen was in front of me. "What the...?"

"I heard you're free now," he told me. "Let's go."

Before I could respond I was lifted into the air and was thrown across one muscular shoulder like a sack of flour. I stared at his broad back in shock, then punched him in the kidney as hard as I could.

"Hey! Put me down asshole!"

He grunted as my blow hit, but only clamped his arm tight around the back of my thighs, holding me close to him. My entire body was on fire from touching him, and my mind was too jumbled to think of a spell to help me get free.

Meanwhile Meri was cracking up like it was the funniest thing she'd ever seen. "I think you've met your match Chamomile. You kids have fun now."

Stephen

Was it wrong of me to practically kidnap my mate? Maybe. But I couldn't find it in me to care. Clearly at least one of her sisters were on my side, and I hoped that would make it easier for me to convince my mate that it was fate that brought us together, not witchcraft. If not, I would just have to tie her to my bed until she saw reason. My wolf rumbled in agreement.

"Where are you taking me?" she asked, wiggling like a fish on a hook and kicking hard against my grip. I could feel the anger rolling off her as she nailed me in the gut with the tip of one shoe. "Let me go right now!"

"Quiet!" I smacked her plump ass in response. She gasped in outrage even while I smelled her arousal. Interesting. My cock twitched in response.

I carried her to my SUV that was parked in the lot near the store. "We're going to my place so we can talk in private," I told her as I unlocked the passenger side door. "Will you sit still, or do I need to get the rope from the trunk?"

Another gasp of outrage. "Fine. Whatever." Her tone was sullen as she sagged back against the seat and crossed her arms.

"Great. Buckle up, Mate. And if you're thinking of running, I'd like to remind you that I have something you don't have."

I paused dramatically and she raised one eyebrow.

"Super human speed."

She rolled her eyes. I quickly closed her door and jogged around to the driver's side, turning on the car and backing out of my parking spot before she could get any more crazy ideas. She was mostly silent on the twenty minute drive to my house, other than a few dramatic sighs. I didn't bother trying to make conversation. I figured it was useless until she calmed down. I knew my actions were heavy-handed, but after a couple of days apart I was desperate to be close to her. Sending her gifts

27

didn't work, so kidnapping her seemed like the next logical step to my lust-addled mind.

I owned a house on the outskirts of a town called Greysden. It was a shifter town, originally founded by grey wolves, but over the years the community had welcomed all manner of shifters from lions to bears to badgers. We even had some bunny shifters. Unlike a lot of shifter towns, there was no ruling alpha or rules about moving in. It was truly a mixed community where everyone was welcome, even the humans who mostly pretended that shifters didn't exist.

I pulled into my driveway and hit the garage door opener. Once I'd safely parked my SUV in the garage, I turned off the engine and went around to open her door. Cami ignored my hand and slid out of the vehicle with a glare that made my cock twitch again. I loved how strong and fiery she was.

I gestured for her to go ahead of me, and she entered the side door into the house. She looked around curiously, taking in the overstuffed dark blue furniture and earth tones on the walls. My place was clean and comfortable, if a bit understated. Cami wandered over to the fireplace and looked at the pictures on the mantle.

"My family," I explained as she picked one photo up to look at it more carefully. "You'll meet them soon. Everyone was very excited when I told them about you." I had a big family with three siblings and a bunch of cousins.

"I agreed to one date, and that's it," she snipped. Her face was flushed and damn if her pissed off face wasn't turning me on. I loved that my mate was a strong woman, and I wasn't afraid to work a little to get her affection.

"Actually, you didn't agree to anything," I reminded her. "That's why I had to take drastic measures."

"All the freaking men in the world and I get this guy?" she mumbled. "Damn my glitchy magic."

"I heard you, and I'll just let you know that I'm a total catch. You're very lucky."

She slammed her hands onto her hips. "Who told you that? Your momma?"

"Among other people," I replied mildly. "How about a drink?"

She sighed. "Do you have any decent beer?"

I went to get us both a beer, grateful for the chance to regroup a bit. I hadn't planned to bring her back here, at least not involuntarily, and I wasn't totally sure what my next move should be. I handed her a beer and nodded at the couch.

"Shall we get to know each other a little bit?"

She sat down without a word.

"Tell me about yourself," I invited. I knew that women usually liked to talk about themselves. I figured if I could get her to open up a bit, she would see how perfect we were for each other.

"Hmm, well, let's see. I like being single, and I don't want to get married or have kids. I like being independent, and I hate being manhandled."

I burst out laughing. "It's funny, but I can tell that even you don't believe what you're saying. Even without wolf's sense of smell I could have scented your arousal when I threw you over my shoulder and smacked your sweet ass."

Cami popped out of her seat. "You're such an asshole."

I stood up and stepped in front of her. "I'm your asshole now."

Before she could respond, I slid my hand behind her head and crashed my lips to hers. I swallowed her gasp and deepened the kiss, pulling her closer to me. I loved the feeling of Cami melting against me as her resistance faded. Her arms slid around my waist, sliding under the hem of my t-shirt to grip the muscles of my lower back.

I took a few steps backwards until the back of my knees hit the couch, then sat down, pulling her on top of me. I readjusted her so that she was straddling me, all without breaking the kiss. At this point I was hard as a rock and Cami was grinding her core against me like she was trying to get herself off through our clothes. I started reciting baseball stats in my head to keep myself from coming in my pants like a teenage boy.

I finally broke the kiss so we could get a breath. Kissing and nibbling down the side of her neck, I sucked on the spot where her neck met her shoulder, imagining how I could place my mark there someday soon. Her hands tightened on my shoulders, and she tilted her head to give me better access. Her breath was coming in small bursts, and I could smell how turned on she was.

My wolf was pushing on me to claim her on the spot, but I reminded him that we needed to be patient with our human mate. I really did want to get to know Cami better before we took the next step. Her stomach growled loudly, catching my attention, and I slowly pulled back to put some space between us. I didn't want to freak her out just when she was softening towards me.

"Are you hungry?"

My mate's eyes were hooded. "Yeah, I could eat." Her stomach growled again, and we both laughed.

"How about I make you dinner?" My wolf chuffed in approval that we would taking care of our mate with food.

"You can cook?" She seemed surprised.

"I have many talents." I shifted her off my lap and stood up, reaching for her hand. "Keep me company while I cook?"

I took it as a victory when she came along without an argument.

Cami

Stephen decided to grill, so we worked together to marinate the meat and prepare some vegetables to barbeque. As we prepped the food, he told me a bit about himself and as I relaxed more, I found myself sharing about myself as well. Despite my concerns about the role of magic in his attraction for me, I felt comfortable with him in a way that didn't usually happen until I'd known someone for a long time. Conversation flowed between us with surprising ease.

"What do you do for a living?" I asked.

"I work at Grey Construction," he explained. "My friend Stuart Grey is the owner. We mostly do home remodels and occasional retail interiors."

"Have you worked there long?"

"About fifteen years," he responded. "It's perfect for me, and I love the work."

"It's great when you find work that's meaningful," I responded. "Too many people I know hate their jobs."

"I know you said that you own Rosewater's." At my nod he asked, "Do you have a set schedule at the store?"

"Not really. I'm there most weekdays but I also fill in nights and weekends depending on where I have holes in the schedule."

"How many people work for you?"

"I have one other full-time person and about six part-timers. And my sisters help out when I need them to. We all grew up working in the store, so even though I'm the sole owner now, it's kind of a given that anyone else in the family will pitch in when we need them."

"It's good that you're close with your sisters. Is it just the three of you?"

I nodded and shared that my parents were currently traveling the world but when they were in town, they stayed at the family home. I followed Stephen out to the deck and held the platter of food while he opened the grill and laid out some charcoal. He opened a can of lighter fluid and I stopped him with a hand on his arm.

"That stuff's toxic," I admonished. "Step back."

He followed my instructions with a curious look. Handing him the platter, I moved closer to the grill and waved my finger towards the charcoal. "*Incindre.*" The charcoal immediately lit up. At least my magic was good enough to start a fire, I thought wryly.

"Nice trick," Stephen told me, leaning forward to plant a quick kiss on the tip of my nose. "Now move away and let the man grill our meat."

I rolled my eyes at his teasing. "Yeah OK, I'll just sit here and enjoy my beer then, grill man."

I watched him as he grilled some ground beef patties and vegetables. He moved with a quiet grace that really appealed to me. It made me wonder about his prowess with other types of activities. Suddenly Stephen's head shot up and he met my eyes, as if he could read my mind. Maybe he could, at least a little bit. I'd read that when a shifter was around their fated mate, a bond formed between them that allowed them to tune into each other's emotions. We hadn't slept together, nor had he marked me, but I could still feel the first tenuous strands of a connection between us. I wondered if it felt stronger to him, since he was a shifter.

We ate dinner on the deck, sitting across from each other at a picnic table situated at one end. The sun was starting to fade as we finished our meal. I couldn't deny that I enjoyed hanging out with Stephen, much more than I'd expected. I'd been so focused on the spell that went sideways that I hadn't really allowed myself to wonder who this man really was. He definitely seemed like a good one. I studied him covertly across the table. His scruff was darker now, almost hiding that cute little dimple in his chin. It made him look a little dangerous.

I licked my lips and heard him groan. In a flash he was on his feet and around the table, dropping on the bench next to me. It never ceased to amaze me how quickly these shifters could move.

"What...?"

I didn't get to finish my sentence before Stephen lowered his head and caught my lips with his. His fingers threaded through my long hair, holding my head in place as he nipped at my lower lip, demanding entrance to my mouth. I opened with a sigh. How could I not? The minute his lips touched mine, everything in my body simultaneously lit up and settled down. It was the strangest feeling.

Stephen's other hand slid down to cup one breast, squeezing it gently. I moaned into his mouth as my nipple hardened painfully. My own hands started traveling, sneaking beneath his tight t-shirt to explore the hard planes of his chest. I was starting to see the appeal of a big, burly guy.

I slid my hand down his stomach until I was able to cup the hard erection that was pressing against his jeans. I'd seen it before, of course, it was on full display the other day when we were in the woods, but having his thickness in the palm of my hand really drove the point home, so to speak, that this was a big guy. I couldn't wait to feel him stretching my channel. That's when I made a decision. It had been way too long since I'd been attracted to a man, and honestly, I missed sex. I pulled away and Stephen looked at me curiously.

"I want you," I told him. "But I need to be clear that that I don't want anything serious. If we do this, it's only for tonight. I don't want a mate."

His eyes darkened then glimmered with the hint of his wolf. "We can talk about the mate thing later," he said, jumping off the bench and pulling me to my feet. "For now, I want dessert."

With one sweep of his long arm, he sent everything on the table crashing to the deck. Plates, bottles, leftovers...it all went flying. Before I could take my next breath, Stephen grabbed me by the waist and lifted me up to lay flat on the table. My heart was racing, and my panties were soaked. Wait, what had I been talking to him about?

I raised to my elbows. "What are you doing?"

"I can't wait another moment to taste you," he growled. Stephen gripped the elastic waistband of my skirt and ripped it down my legs, taking my panties with it and leaving me bare. He tossed my clothes over his shoulder and stared down at my glistening pussy with a look that was pure desire.

I felt a thrill. Never in my life had anyone been so overcome with passion for me like this. I'd had relationships of course, and I'd always enjoyed sex, but this felt very different. Before I could think about why that was, Stephen dropped to his knees, pulled my ass closer to the edge of the table, and threw my legs over his shoulders. Thank the Goddess the table was sealed wood, or I would have gotten a very unfortunate splinter in my ass.

Stephen growled something that sounded suspiciously like "Mine!" before lowering his head. His rough tongue slid through my wet folds, lapping up my essence and building my excitement. I shuddered as he licked up and down a few times before turning his full attention to my throbbing clit.

Stephen tapped his tongue against the sensitive bundle of nerves, then circled a few times before resuming the tapping motion. I gasped as he inserted one thick finger into my channel, slowly pumping in and out. I rolled my head from side to side, rocking my hips against his face to encourage him to get closer to where I needed him. I heard him chuckle against me. He slipped a second finger inside me, curling his fingers to find my G-spot. At the same time, he lowered his head and sucked my clit between his lips. That was all it took for me to come completely undone. I trembled under the force of my orgasm, clamping my thighs tighter against his head and gasping as wave after wave of pleasure shook my body.

"Fuck," I gasped as I came down from the waves of pleasure.

Stephen's head popped up, licking his lips. "Mmm. Delicious."

I felt a wave of heat rise up my face. I enjoyed oral as much as the next girl, but I'd never been so shameless, never come so loudly and quickly. What had gotten into me?

"Oh no." Stephen pushed to his feet and slid me farther up the picnic table before crawling up to trap me under his bulky body. He pushed up on his elbows so he could look down at me.

"Oh no?" I asked in confusion. "What?"

"Don't start thinking," he commanded, his voice a deep growl.

"Um..."

"I want you so bad Cami," he interrupted. "Please don't make me wait any longer."

I couldn't help but giggle. "Longer?" I asked. "We've known each other for like forty-eight hours."

"That's forever to a shifter who's found his mate," he said solemnly.

"What are you waiting for then?" I asked softly. "Take me."

His eyes widened, then he slid off the table, shucked his pants, and before I knew what was happening, he was back between my legs, notching his thick cock between my folds.

"Are you sure?" he asked. I could see a hint of his canines lengthening with excitement.

I nodded. "Just don't bite me, Wolfie. I meant it when I said this was only for one night."

Stephen slid into me in one long, hard thrust, making us both gasp. I felt so full I could hardly breathe. He leaned down, kissing me deeply as he gave me some time to adjust. The minute the grip of my internal muscles relaxed, he started moving, sliding in and out in a rhythm that I quickly matched. I wrapped my legs around his waist, tilting my pelvis and pulling him deeper.

"You feel so good, Mate," he ground out. "I can't believe we finally found each other."

I slid my hands up beneath the shirt he was still wearing, and ran my nails up his strong back, scoring the skin. He hissed at the sensation, picking up the pace. There was nothing tentative in his movements, like there often was when you were with someone for the first time. With every thrust Stephen pushed so deep inside me that it was impossible to know where he ended and I started. It was heavenly. I could feel my body tightening as another orgasm crashed down on me.

"Stephen!" I gasped.

He lowered his head to the crook of my neck, pounding into me for all he was worth. As my inner muscles squeezed around him, he let himself go, coming with a long groan of masculine satisfaction. I felt the heat of his cum filling me up before he collapsed on top of me, panting harshly against my shoulder. I shivered beneath him. We stayed still for a long time. I thought he might have fallen asleep, but he finally lifted his head and pressed a soft kiss against my lips.

"That was incredible Mate, but we still have a lot of night left."

Stephen

When I dropped Cami off at her house the next morning, I could swear she was walking funny. And why wouldn't she? We'd made love so many times last night I'd lost count. We'd barely gotten any sleep at all, and I knew that a full day of manual labor today was going to be challenging. Cami wasn't the only one with sore muscles this morning, but it had definitely been worth it.

I'd made good progress with my mate last night and although she still didn't want me to mark her, I knew she was softening to me. And not just because I gave her about a dozen orgasms. It was the connection we'd felt, the way we'd talked softly as we rested between rounds of lovemaking. In the darkness of night, we'd both opened up to each other, talking until we could barely stay awake.

Don't get me wrong, it had been a struggle holding my wolf back from marking her and claiming her in the way only a shifter could. But he'd been comforted by spending the night together and feeling the mate bond growing stronger between us even without my marking her.

I'd been expecting Cami to pull away in the morning but while she'd been pretty quiet on the ride over to her house, she hadn't totally withdrawn. I called that a win, even though she refused to commit to getting together again.

"Remember what I said? One night only Stephen."

Her words had lacked conviction though. I'd walked her to her door and kissed her senseless on the porch, feeling a surge of masculine pride when she stumbled into her house looking dazed.

I rolled into work with a satisfied smile on my face. My boss Stuart immediately noticed my unusually cheerful demeanor.

"What happened?" he asked suspiciously. "It's not like you to be so happy in the morning."

It was true. I was not a morning person. If I didn't have to work, I would stay up late and sleep in every morning.

"I found my mate," I told him proudly.

He raised his eyebrows. "Wow, that's great man. Congratulations. Tell me about her while we lay the kitchen tile."

I told Stuart the whole story as we worked side by side. We'd been friends for a long time, and I knew that he'd had some challenges convincing his mate Kat to accept him as her mate. Even though she was a tiger shifter and understood all about fated mates, she and Stuart had a bit of a bumpy road to their happily ever after.

"She thinks a shifter would fall under a love spell?" he snorted. "We're stronger minded than that."

"It doesn't matter, it's what she believes," I explained.

"Well, you'll just have to change her mind." He shot me a smirk. "Lots of orgasms are effective."

I rolled my eyes. "I already gave her that last night, but there's still a wall between us. And when I suggested getting together again tonight, she told me that she was too busy to date anyone. She said even though last night was quote 'fun', she didn't want to see me again."

That part stung, I had to admit, even though when Cami said it, she seemed to be trying to convince herself as much as me.

"Well, you'll just need to break those walls down," Stuart told me, as if it was the easiest thing in the world.

"How?"

"Start by seeing if you can get her family and friends on your side."

I thought about Stuart's words for the rest of the morning. On my lunch break I poked around on social media until I found Cami's sister Pepper. Given that she was the one Cami was most worried about, I wanted to see if I could get her on my side. I sent her a message asking to meet and, to my surprise, she agreed. She didn't want to meet in their town in case we ran into Cami, so we agreed to get a drink at Murphy's Bar here in Greysden.

Pepper was already sitting at one of the high tops when I got there. I greeted our waitress Marie and ordered a beer. Murphy's Bar was an institution in this town, and the wolf shifter had worked here at Murphy's since she was in high school. We'd all thought she would leave town when the original owner, Murph, died, but then his son Ben had inherited the bar. To everyone's surprise, the bear shifter from New York City was her mate. Like so many of my friends, they'd had a bit of a rocky road to happily ever after, but they now appeared to be blissfully happy. The sassy wolf and serious bear made a great couple.

"What did you want to talk to me about?" Pepper asked, sucking on a straw dipped into what looked like some kind of fruity blended drink. She seemed friendly, not at all upset about what happened with the spell, so I took that as a good sign.

"I need your help."

Pepper shot me an amused look. "Ah yeah, I suspected that was it. Cami giving you some trouble?"

I nodded. "I mean, we had a great night together last night..."

"Yeah Meri told me that you carried Cami out of the store yesterday like a caveman," she laughed. "Given that she didn't come home until this morning, we figured things had gone well."

"They did go well, but she's still resistant to the idea of being mates. I know part of it is that she thinks you're mad about her messing up the spell, but it feels like more than that."

Pepper nodded. "Yeah, my sister is a stubborn one, and she's always said she wanted to be single. Even when she was a kid. But I think you'll win her over if you're patient. I know that's not in your shifter DNA, but she's going to need time to get used to the idea of being mates. Don't worry though, Meri and I are in your corner. We've talked about this, and we both agree that we just want our sister to be happy, and we think she'll be happy with you. We'll do whatever we can to make that happen."

She took another long draw of her drink. "Just promise me you'll treat her right. She's had some asshole boyfriends in the past."

My wolf growled deep inside at the idea of someone hurting our mate. Or touching her. I knew going into last night that she wasn't a virgin or anything – she was in her late thirties after all—but it was best if I didn't think about the guys who came before me.

"I'll treat her like the princess she is," I vowed.

Cami's sister snorted. "Yeah, princess, that describes my sister. Did you guys make plans to see each other again?"

I shook my head and glumly took a sip of my beer. "No, I couldn't pin her down on getting together again. She says she's too busy for me."

"Well, if she's going to be stubborn, you're just going to need to be a stray cat."

"Stray cat?"

"You know how stray cats come around and then if you feed them, they keep coming around and the next thing you know, you kind of have a cat even though you really didn't want one?"

"No, not really. I'm a wolf, remember? Cats don't really like our kind."

Pepper sighed deeply and muttered something under her breath that sounded like, *idiot men*.

"What I mean is, you need to keep showing up wherever she is, insinuating yourself into her life until she can't remember not having you there. And turn up the smolder." She looked at me critically. "You're a charming enough guy, make her swoon."

"Swoon?" I asked in confusion.

Pepper sighed again. "Build up the tension. Stay close to her. Give her a lot of innocent touches, or maybe flirt with another woman and make her jealous, that kind of thing. Be charming and flirty and stay in her orbit, and you'll make her go crazy wanting you. But don't put out again without a commitment."

"Are you saying I should withhold sex?"

"You need to do whatever it takes to make her so desperate that she'll agree to be your mate."

I frowned, feeling slightly insulted. "Are you saying she would have to be desperate to be with me?"

Pepper waved at Marie. "Good Goddess, I'm going to need another drink. You're even more hopeless than I thought."

Cami

The door to the shop opened just before closing time. I wasn't surprised to see it was Stephen. I didn't need to be my psychic sister to figure out he'd turn up eventually. Not that I could blame him. Last night had been phenomenal. I could have happily stayed in bed with Stephen until we both died of hunger. He was that good.

But once I'd gotten away from the overwhelming pull of hormones, I'd realized what a huge mistake it had been to sleep with him. It was going to be way harder to keep him at a distance now that I knew how explosive things were between us. *You agreed to one night only,* I reminded myself.

"Mate." He pulled me into a long hug. I breathed in his scent and allowed myself to relax into him for a long moment before pulling away. Damn he smelled good. This close to him, I had a hard time remembering why I was supposed to be avoiding him.

"What are you doing here?" I asked, forcing myself to sound irate even though part of me was happy to see him. "I told you I wasn't free tonight." I'd lied, but he didn't need to know that.

"I'm just looking for a book."

"What kind of book?" I asked suspiciously.

"How to please a woman."

I choked on my own spit. "I think you could probably write that book."

He gave me a sexy smirk. "It never hurts to study up on new techniques."

I sighed. "Look in aisle five."

To my surprise he ambled off to find a book instead of staying near me. Hmm, maybe he'd finally gotten the message that I wasn't interested. I continued working, one eye on Stephen the whole time. He was acting like just another guy looking for a book. That was weird.

I had just made the announcement that the store was closing when he came up to the counter with several books.

"Find what you need?" I asked in my professional voice.

He looked amused, but just said, "Yes thank you."

I rang up his books. "That'll be thirty-four twenty-three."

He handed me his credit card, his hand brushing against mine just a moment too long. I swear it was enough for me to dampen my panties. What was it about this guy? I'd never been this horny in my life. I swear I wanted to throw him on the floor and ride him right here in my store. Holding myself back with effort, I finished his transaction and slid the card on the counter towards him, carefully avoiding touching him again. He grabbed his books and receipt and gave me a casual smile.

"Thanks, see you later." And then he was gone.

What the hell? What happened to the pushy shifter who'd badgered me all morning about getting together again? Had he changed his mind about me already? Maybe last night wasn't as good as I thought. I had a feeling I was going to have a long night with my vibrator after this encounter.

The next couple of days it seemed like I ran in to Stephen everywhere I went. The coffee shop. The grocery store. The gas station. I even ran into him when I was at the bank. When I saw him waiting in line at the ATM behind me, I'd had enough.

"What are you doing here?" I asked. My hands came to my hips, and I gave him my best glare.

He nodded at the debit card in his hand. "Getting some cash."

"You don't even live in this town," I reminded him. "I'm sure they have stores and banks in Greysden. Don't think I don't know what you're doing."

"What am I doing?" he asked with studied innocence.

I rolled my eyes. "You're trying to convince me to go out with you again."

"I haven't even called or texted you," he protested. "I can't help it if this is a small town."

I stepped closer and jabbed him in the chest with my finger. "Leave me alone."

He grabbed my hand and engulfed it in his much larger hand. I could feel the work-roughened skin against my softer skin, and it reminded me of how much I loved having those hands on other parts of my body. My nipples hardened and I felt a flush of arousal. When his nostrils flared and he got that irritating smirk on his face, I knew he smelled my body's reaction, which just pissed me off more. Shooting him another glare, I stalked away. I ignored the twinge in my chest as I put distance between us.

When I got home from work that, both of my sisters were there in the living room. It wasn't unheard of for the three of us to be home at the same time, we all lived together after all, but with our busy schedules, it wasn't an everyday occurrence either.

"Ah, there she is. Welcome home, big sister."

I looked at Pepper suspiciously. "What?"

She shot me an innocent look. "Nothing. Just welcoming you home Chamomile. Meri and I were thinking that we might go out for dinner or something. Do you want to join us?"

"Only if I get to pick the place."

I didn't trust my sisters not to try to manufacture some coincidental meeting with Stephen. They had both been driving me crazy all week, pushing me to give him a chance. What they didn't understand was that as much as I was tempted, I couldn't let myself get close. There was no way I was willing to let myself be vulnerable around a man. After the disastrous end of my last relationship, I'd promised myself I'd stay single. I promised myself no one would ever hurt me again.

I'd met Frank at a booksellers' conference in Denver. He was a few years older than me, tall and handsome and charming. The attraction between us was strong and immediate. We'd fallen into bed hours after we met, and we got pretty serious pretty fast. My parents still owned the store at the time, giving me a lot more free time to go on long walks and spend lazy weekend days snuggling with someone who seemed perfect for me.

The verbal abuse was subtle when it started. The off-hand comments about my weight. The "joke" that my sisters got "all the beauty" in the family and I was lucky he hadn't met one of them first. The snarky comments about nepotism, implying that I hadn't earned my position as store manager of our family business. Frank gradually chipped away at my self-esteem over the course of our time together and yet some part of me thought he was the best I could get. He acted like I should be pathetically grateful that he wanted to be with me, and gradually I started to believe it myself. My sisters both actively hated him, but I convinced myself that they were just jealous that I had someone in my life when they didn't. I should have realized that my sisters were much better than that.

I don't know how long I would have let him manipulate me, but everything came to a head one night about six months after we started dating. We had made plans for us to meet at his place, and when he wasn't there at the appointed time, I let myself in with my key. When he didn't show up, I texted and called him, worried that he'd been in a car accident or something. He'd finally come home several hours later, super drunk and belligerent. He was upset because he'd lost his job as a regional manager for a large retail bookstore chain because he hadn't been meeting his sales goals.

I knew enough about his work ethic to understand that his employer had found out about his long lunches and frequent absences, but somehow Frank decided it was my fault.

"You made me lose my job," he'd raged at me as soon as he returned home.

"Me? How would I do that?" I'd protested.

"You're too needy. Too distracting. I'm so busy dealing with you and all your neuroses that I can't concentrate on my job. You've always been jealous that I have a better job than you, one I actually earned instead of getting it from Mommy and Daddy."

I couldn't believe it. Not only were his words mean, but they were also completely untrue. He'd complained many times over the course of our relationship that I didn't have enough time for him. He resented any time I spent with family and friends. I'd finally had enough, and I spoke up to him for the first time in our relationship.

"Oh no," I'd yelled back. "You don't get to put all that on me. If you lost your job, it's because of your poor performance, not because of me."

That's when he hit me, right in the face. As I'd stumbled back and hit the wall, I couldn't believe it. I'd never been struck in my life before, other than the silly little slap fights my sisters and I had when we were younger and would get upset with each other.

I'd been filled with rage, a rage so strong that it focused my magic in a way that had never happened before. As Frank advanced on me, presumably to hit me again, I'd waved my hand and used my magic to fling him back through the air. He'd landed on the floor with a grunt, shock clearly etched on his face.

"What the fuck?"

One thing I'd never shared with Frank: that I was a witch. He started to get up, and I used the force of my magic to pin him to the floor, where he wiggled like a bug who couldn't turn over. I sent a prayer of thanks to the Goddess that my magic was working when I really needed it.

"Who the hell are you?"

"The woman who is done with you." I'd hissed. "Don't ever come near me again, or I'll make you regret it."

It had taken everything in me not to kick him as I walked by him, still pinned to the floor by my magic.

"Baby, wait," he'd whined. "I didn't mean to hurt you, I'm just so upset about my job."

I didn't even answer him as I ran out of his house for the last time. He'd badgered me for months, calling and texting and sending gifts and showing up at work. The more I resisted him, the more persistent he became. It was Meri who finally got rid of him for good. She'd came home while he was pounding on the front door, screaming for me to come outside and talk to him. Frank had turned around to try to charm her when she suddenly got one of her psychic flashes. Grabbing her head with one hand, she clutched his arm with her other.

"Miguel is coming for you," she'd intoned, her voice strong and clear. "He's angry. He wants his money for the drugs you stole from him. He's on his way."

For once, Meri's psychic abilities had worked in our favor. I'd had no idea that he was doing drugs, but Frank had turned so white at her words I could see it from the front window. Giving Meri a panicked look, he'd pulled away from her and ran to his car. That was the last we'd seen of him.

I didn't think that Stephen would behave like Frank. He was the complete opposite of him in many ways. Yet I still couldn't trust whatever was happening between us. I needed to stay away from him no matter how much I yearned to be close to him. I had learned the hard way that I could only rely on myself. No matter how compelling the wolf shifter was, I needed to stay strong.

Stephen

I hadn't seen my mate in two days, and it was making my wolf edgy. I couldn't eat, I couldn't sleep, and I couldn't stop thinking about Cami. We'd been short-handed at work, and I'd wound up putting in two consecutive twelve-hour days to help us keep on schedule. I'd scarcely had time to do more than work and sleep. Normally I didn't mind helping out and working extra hours, but knowing that my mate was out there in world unclaimed was driving my wolf crazy.

I debated heading over to see if I could find her in town but decided to wait until the next day. It was Friday night, and I had all weekend to woo my mate. My wolf was dying to go for a run, and despite my fatigue I figured it would be a good idea to wear him out a bit, so he'd quit bugging me about finding Cami.

I'd been messaging with her sister Pepper, getting intel on Cami's schedule so I could turn up when she least expected me. It was dishonest and maybe a bit stalkerish, but desperate times called for desperate measures. My phone rang with a text just as I was stripping down on my back porch. My house backed up against the forest, giving me great access to the wild areas that ringed Greysden. Since most of the people in town was shifters, it wasn't unusual to see someone wandering around in their animal form. Or coming home from a shift stark naked. I pulled out my phone.

Pepper: *We're having dinner on the patio at Ellery's if you want to drop by.*

Me: *Got it. Thanks.*

I was tempted to get dressed again and drive over to Ellery's, but decided a more subtle approach was warranted. In my wolf form, I could keep an eye on her without her knowing about it. I jumped off the porch, shifting mid-air. I felt the familiar pain of bones and muscles lengthening and changing shape as my canines pushed through my gums and my tail extended from the bottom of my spine. By the time my paws touched the grass, I was wearing my fur and eager to run. I let my wolf take control; he knew was to do.

Ellery's was about ten or twelve miles away from my house, and my wolf made quick work of running through the woods towards the restaurant. In this form, I could easily reach speeds of twenty-five to thirty miles an hour. I came out of the woods near Ellery's about fifteen minutes later. Sniffing the air, I quickly located my mate. The restaurant had a huge outdoor patio that was separated from the woods by an expanse of wild grass. I kept low, trying to avoid attracting too much attention. Keeping my eyes on my mate, I stalked closer.

I could tell the exact minute she realized I was there. Cami stiffened, then turned to scan the grass. Her eyes went right to where I was sneaking through the high grass. I'd felt the mate bond forming, the mystical connection between a shifter and their true mate, but I hadn't realized that she was feeling it too. She looked annoyed as she shot me a glare, then turned and said something to her sisters, both of whom shrugged with forced casualness.

I'd meant to watch her from afar, but my wolf wasn't having it. He wanted to get closer. He needed to get closer. Since Cami had already spotted me, I figured there was no use in hiding in the grass. Someone at a neighboring table gasped as I jumped lightly onto the patio, heading towards my mate.

"It's OK," Pepper called to her. "That's just our dog. He must have gotten out of the car."

"That's not a dog, it's a wolf," the lady protested. Sniffing the air, I realized she was human. Humans knew about shifters, but most of them were in denial. As shifters, we didn't flaunt our dual natures, and in return, most of the humans pretended that we didn't exist. It worked out fine for all of us.

"Yeah, we get that a lot," Pepper said, turning to me. "But wolves can't do this. Sit Stephen."

I dropped to my haunches, sitting down, and trying to make myself look small and unthreatening.

"Lay down."

Pepper pointed to the ground near their table, and I settled onto my stomach, paws under my muzzle as I stared at my mate. She studiously avoided my gaze.

"Good boy," Pepper said in that voice women used on animals. Internally I rolled my eyes, but I appreciated the assist. I hadn't thought it through when I decided to run over here wearing my fur.

Just then the waiter came by, giving me a disapproving frown. "No dogs on the porch, ladies."

"We were just leaving," Meri assured him. "Pepper, pay the check while Cami and I take Stephen to the car." She stood up and patted her leg. "Come on boy, let's go home and get your kibble."

This time it was Cami who rolled her eyes. I followed her and Meri to the car, and when Meri opened the back seat, I didn't wait for an invitation; I hopped right into the car.

"What are you doing?" Cami protested. "Run along now, Wolfie. You can't come with us."

I didn't move. Pepper came up and slid into the passenger seat before Cami could get there, forcing my mate to get in the backseat with me. She sighed deeply as she settled herself into the seat next to me. As soon as Meri started the car, I shifted forward to rest my head on her lap. To my surprise, Cami reached up and rubbed that spot between my ears that felt so good. The next thing I knew, I was fast asleep.

My mate stirring beneath my head woke me up. Her look was almost tender as she looked down at me.

"You're worn out, aren't you?"

It was obvious that she could sense my deep exhaustion through the mate bond. I nodded my wolf head, telling myself it was a good sign that she cared.

"All right then, you might as well come in for a while. I'm too tired to drive you back to Greysden, and I'm thinking you're too tired to run back yet." She pointed at me and gave me a stern look. "No funny business."

My wolf started panting excitedly as we jumped out of the car to follow our mate. The sun was setting, and there was a bit of a chill in the air as we walked into the house. Meri and Pepper were standing in the entryway, obviously spying on us. They looked gleeful.

"Why don't you take your boyfriend upstairs?" Pepper suggested with a mischievous look in her eyes.

I didn't wait for Cami to argue, I just padded upstairs. I heard her whispering with her sisters as I sniffed the floor and followed her scent to her bedroom. My mate came up behind me as I crossed over to the bed.

"What are you doing, Wolfie?"

Ignoring her, I hopped up on the bed, turned in a circle a couple of times, then laid down. Her bed was soft and comfortable, and it smelled like her. My wolf was in heaven. My eyes grew heavy again.

She sighed deeply. "OK, here's the deal. You can stay here tonight, but you need to stay in your wolf form so we're not tempted to do anything more than sleep. No sexy times for you, mister. I mean it."

I wagged my tail and snuggled into the comforter. I couldn't help but wonder who she was trying to keep away from temptation: me or her.

Cami went into the en-suite bathroom and returned a few minutes later wearing a pair of sweatpants and a giant sweatshirt that fell almost to her knees. I immediately felt a rush of jealousy as I wondered if she'd gotten the sweatshirt from one of her boyfriends. I was tempted to shift back to human to ask her about it, but honestly, I was just too exhausted. It was like I'd been on high alert the entire time we'd been separated, and now that we were together again, the adrenaline rush faded, and I was so sleepy I couldn't keep my eyes open.

Cami settled on the bed next to me, slipping underneath the covers and leaning against the headboard. She grabbed a remote control from the bedside table and switched on the television that was mounted to the wall.

"I'm going to share a deep, dark secret with you," she said. "I like to watch Scottish time travel romances." She started an on-demand video of a popular TV show, then reached over to rub my back. Before the opening credits finished, I was fast asleep again.

Cami

I woke up sweating. Was I getting night sweats already? I thought I had a couple of more years before menopause hit. I realized with a start that something was pressed against my back. Something big and warm and furry. It all came back to me. Dinner on the patio. Stephen popping up in the grass, then pretending to be a dog. Snuggling against his warm body as I watched my recorded shows until I fell asleep. Waking up next to Stephen in his wolf form was almost as fabulous as waking up next to him as a human. Minus the morning wood, of course.

After heading into the bathroom to pee and brush my teeth, I returned to find that Stephen had switched back into his human form and was reclining on the bed buck naked. Speaking of morning wood...

"What are you doing?" I asked. My voice was scratchy from sleep.

"Nothing," Stephen replied as he lazily scratched his chest. My eyes followed the movement. Damn these shifters aged well. I knew Stephen was forty, but he had the body of a twenty year old. A very hot, very fit twenty year old. Yum. My panties were immediately soaked, and I could tell by the smirk on his face and the flare of his nostrils that Stephen was well aware of that fact.

He crooked a finger at me, and without thinking I followed his unspoken command. As soon as I got close enough, he reached out his hand and pulled me towards the bed, rolling me onto my back underneath him before I even realized what had happened.

"What are you doing?" I asked again.

Stephen's smile was pure sin. "This."

His head descended slowly, giving me enough time to push him away. I knew I should, but I just couldn't do it. Not when I wanted to kiss him more than I wanted my next breath. After our night together I'd freaked out and pushed him away. What had happened with Frank made me doubt that I was a good judge of men anymore. But now, now I was tired of denying myself what I really wanted. Stephen. I knew logically that it was the magic spell bringing us together, but it felt so real to me.

His lips met mine, soft but firm, and I felt everything in my body relax. *This one.* I heard the words rumble through my body and in that moment, I let go of all of my reservations and kissed him back passionately. At least until I heard the pounding on the door.

"Chamomile? Honey, are you in there?"

I stiffened beneath Stephen. "Oh crap!"

Stephen was immediately on high alert. "Who is that? What's happening?"

I groaned. So much for my morning delight. "It's my mother. She's come home to reverse the love spell for us."

Stephen reared back, a flash of hurt passing through his eyes. "What?"

I rolled out from underneath him as my mother continued to pound on the door. "Hang on Mom," I called. "I'll be right out."

I turned back to explain to Stephen, "When I first realized that the spell had gone wrong, I emailed my mother to ask her to come home and fix it. I didn't want us to be bound because of a spell that was meant to help someone else. She and my father were traveling, Goddess knows where, so when I didn't hear back from her right away, I forgot all about it. I'm sure that's why she's here."

He pushed to his feet, his expression a mixture of disbelief and betrayal. "You asked another witch to undo our bond?"

I shook my head vigorously. "No, well, yes, kind of. I wanted to know if what we were feeling was because of the spell or if it was fate, like you say it is. I wanted to know if it was real."

"Is it really that bad being my mate that you have to use magic to make it go away? God, Cami. Were you even going to tell me about this?"

I'd never seen Stephen look so upset. I reached for him, but he backed away, heading for the door. "I can't believe you would do this to me, I can't believe you would do this to us."

He opened the door, nodding at my mother who shot him a wide-eyed look as she took in his naked body. A second later I heard his bare feet pounding down the stairs, quickly followed by the sound of the front door slamming as he ran out of the house. And out of my life, no doubt. My mother was here to fix this mess now. Once the spell was reversed, I had no doubt in my mind that the overwhelming connection we felt would be gone. And when the connection was gone, that would be it for us.

I pressed my hand against my mouth as my eyes filled with tears for the first time in years. Everything between us had just been the magic, I reminded myself. He'd never been mine to keep. Flinging myself into my mother's arms, I started to sob. My mother smoothed my hair, whispering words of comfort until I'd cried myself out, then grabbed my hand and pulled me to sit on the bottom of the bed.

"That was the guy? The wolf shifter who came after the spell and thinks you're his mate?"

I nodded.

"Why the tears, Chamomile? I thought you wanted out of this spell?"

"I did, but now I'm not so sure. I...I think I love him, but I'm not sure if it's genuine or I'm just wrapped up in the spell."

My mother shook her head. "What does it matter? If it's the spell, or if it's the call of the shifter's fated mate, it's all magic Chamomile. Love is its own magic."

"But the magic was meant for Pepper."

"The magic was meant for whomever it would serve most at this time. Clearly that was you."

"I can't live the rest of my life wondering if the man I love is with me because of free will, or because of some magic spell."

"You really love that wolf, don't you?" she asked.

I sniffed and felt the truth rush through me. "Yes."

"And yet you want to take a chance on the reversal spell making all that go away?"

"I guess, I mean, I think I do."

She raised one eyebrow, the same way she'd done when I was a child and said something ridiculous.

"I just need to know for sure Mom. I don't want to spend the rest of my life doubting his feelings for me." I didn't add that I had no doubt about my own feelings. They were real, and they would last even if he forgot all about me. I knew that as sure as I knew my own name.

Mom sighed deeply. "From what I've heard, there's nothing to doubt. But if you really want me to do a reversal, I can." She rubbed my shoulder. "But don't blame me if the magic doesn't work the way you hope it will."

Stephen

I ran through the woods as fast as my paws could carry me. My muscles bunched and lengthened as I flew past the trees headed for Greysden. For home.

Home is where Cami is, my wolf rebuked me.

"She doesn't want to be with us," I reminded us both. "That's why she wants her mother to undo her stupid love spell."

The betrayal hurt so much I could scarcely breathe. We had connected. I hadn't imagined that. And last night, something had shifted between us. As I lay curled up next to her in my wolf form, I could feel her resistance fading. I could feel the love in her touch as she absently stroked my fur while she watched her ridiculous TV shows. And when I'd awoken in the middle of the night, she had been curled around me, her head resting on my side as she slept peacefully.

What would happen after Mrs. Rosewater did the reversal spell, I wondered. Would I feel the same? Would she? Would we go back to being strangers living in neighboring towns, never knowing the other existed?

It's not a spell, she is our mate.

I hoped my wolf was right. Even if I forgot that Cami existed, I would still miss her on a cellular level. The connection with her was burned into my very soul. Even though I hadn't bitten her and claimed her, even though our mate bond hadn't been sealed yet, it was still there. It wouldn't be severed. Not completely.

If by some chance the spell actually broke the bond, I knew instinctively that I'd never be able to even look at another woman. The fates only brought one true mate for every shifter. Even if we didn't remember each other, I'd still mourn her loss. I would be doomed to spend the rest of my life all alone.

Not all alone, my wolf reminded me. My wolf sent me a series of images, like pictures in my mind. Me and Cami snuggled together in bed. A wedding ceremony in the clearing where we first met. The two of us sitting on the couch reading, both of us old and grey. I didn't know if the images were wishful thinking or some kind of a vision of the future, but they gave me comfort.

"I hope you're right buddy."

By the time I got home, I was panting from the exertion of running full out for so long. I burst out of the woods into my back yard, making a beeline for my porch. I was running so fast I almost didn't notice the figure sitting on my back steps. Cami. I skidded to a stop, wondering if I was hallucinating.

Cami raised her hand in a half-hearted wave. I stalked towards her, watching her carefully. Her eyes were red and swollen. Clearly she had been crying. I exhaled sharply and called forth my human form. My fur receded, quickly followed by my claws and fangs, and my body reformed into my smaller human shape. I landed on my hands and knees in the grass, a few feet from my mate, breathing hard.

"What are you doing here?" I gasped.

"Can we talk for a few minutes?" she asked. "Please."

I walked past her on the porch and opened the back door, gesturing for her to follow me in. "I'll be right back."

I was dripping with sweat after my hard run, so I headed into the bathroom for a quick shower. The truth was, I needed some space too. If she was here to break it off, I needed to be prepared. After my shower, I brushed my teeth and pulled on some clothes, returning to find Cami in the living room. She was sitting on the couch, nervously twisting her hands in her lap. I plopped down on the other side of the couch, keeping distance between us, and remained silent, waiting for her to talk.

I couldn't decide how I was feeling. I'd been so hurt and betrayed by her plan to reverse the spell, even though I didn't believe that magic was involved in our connection. Not witch's magic anyway. Shifter magic was fated, and totally different. At least I hoped so. Honestly, it was her lack of faith that hurt me the most. But I also felt a sharp stab of fear. If I was wrong and Cami was right, I was about to lose my fated mate. Just the thought of it made me want to burrow into a hole and lick my metaphorical wounds.

"I told my mother I didn't want her to reverse the spell."

My head popped up to stare at my mate in shock. "Why not?"

She scooted closer and I inhaled her sweet scent.

"I don't want to risk losing you," she whispered. "Even if we forgot all about each other, I still would miss you. The thing is...I love you, Stephen. I don't know if it's the spell or your shifter magic or just plain old human emotion. And I don't care. The only thing I care about is you, and us, and our future together." Her eyes filled with tears as she added, "That is, if you're still interested in a future with me."

My heart filled with joy, but I knew what I had to do...

"We're going through with the reversal spell," I said firmly, surprising both of us.

"What?"

"When I claim you as my mate – and make no mistake I will be claiming you, and soon – I don't want that damn spell hanging over our heads for the rest of our lives. I don't want you or anyone else to ever doubt that what we have is real, that we were brought together by fate, not by some stupid spell."

"But what if the spell breaks the connection between us?"

"That's a risk I'm willing to take Cami. I'm willing to risk it all because I know, in the end, we will be together, and you will be mine. And when your mother is done with the spell, you'll know it too. Then there will be no doubts remaining between us."

An hour later I was back at Cami's house. Mrs. Rosewater led the way to the clearing in the woods where I first ran into the sisters. Pepper and Meri walked side by side behind her, with me and Cami bringing up the rear. We walked hand-in-hand, and I could feel her start to tremble the closer we got.

Once we got there, I stood to the side while Cami's mom drew a circle in the dirt and placed various herbs and crystals in front of her. Pepper stacked some twigs, and her mom started a small fire with a flick of her wrist.

"I'm ready. You can all come to the circle now."

We gathered around the fire, sitting within the lines drawn in the dirt. Cami took one of my hands while Pepper took the other. Meri gasped loudly as Pepper grabbed her with her other hand.

"What is it?" Pepper asked. "What do you see?"

Meri rubbed her forehead, her eyes going glassy as a vision flashed in her mind. "A monster!"

We all stared at her as she mumbled incoherently for a few seconds. Her gaze cleared and she stared at her sister in shock. "Pepper! Your true love is a monster!"

"What are you talking about?" Pepper grabbed her hand again and squeezed. "Are you saying I'm going to fall in love with a terrible person? What the hell? Why do I have such bad luck in this damn clearing?"

"I don't know." Meri shook her head, as if clearing it. "I saw you in my vision, we were all in the library, and you were telling us you were in love, but he was a monster. It's all kind of hazy."

Pepper looked disturbed. "Oh for Goddess's sake, can we just get on with this spell reversal so I can go home and have a drink?"

Mrs. Rosewater looked between her daughters thoughtfully, but didn't pry anymore. We all fell silent as she began to chant the magical incantations while she scattered ingredients into the fire. After a few moments, she pulled out a small vial with a green liquid in it and slid it towards Pepper.

"Drink this. It should flush the other potion out of your body."

The sisters looked at their mother in confusion. "Potion?" Pepper asked. "What potion?"

"The potion your sister gave you when she did the spell," Mrs. Rosewater explained.

"I didn't give her anything to drink," Cami said.

Pepper nodded. "Yeah, she just did the smoky herbs thing you're doing, right Meri?"

Meri nodded in confirmation. Mrs. Rosewater sat back on her heels and started to laugh. We all looked at each other, even more confused.

"What's so funny?" Cami asked her mother.

"You didn't complete the spell."

"I don't understand."

"You only did the first part of the spell Chamomile. It's like you knocked at the door but didn't go inside."

I raised my hand like I was in school. "Can you explain that more clearly for the non-magical folks here please?"

Mrs. Rosewater pinned me with an intense look. "The first part of the spell creates an environment where the participants are receptive. It's a heart opening spell. But for it to also bring love, the person who wants to be matched needs to also drink the love potion. No love potion, no love spell."

She turned her gaze to her oldest daughter. "The magic softened your heart Chamomile, but Stephen came to you because of fate, not because of the spell."

I pumped my fist in the air like I'd just scored the winning touchdown in the Super Bowl. "Told you!" I crowed to Cami. "Shifter magic for the win!"

I leapt to my feet, dragging her up with me, then tossed her over my shoulder like I'd done that day I'd spirited her away from her store.

"What are you doing?" she laughed as I took off running. I tightened my arm around her thighs to keep her from falling off.

"We're going home Cami. I'm not going to waste another day without my mate mark on your neck."

"But..."

I smacked her ass smartly. "No more excuses Chamomile Ginseng Rosewater. Tonight, you will be mine."

And she was.

Epilogue—Cami

Four months later...

"Happy anniversary!"

I looked around at all the people gathering in the backyard at Rosewater manor. It seemed like the whole town had come out to celebrate my parents' fortieth anniversary. My sister Meri had outdone herself planning this party; she had always loved organizing social events. The yard had been completely transformed into a party venue with long tables laden with food, a seating area, games for the kids, even a dance floor.

"Thank you," Mom said, leaning into to wrap me and Stephen into a warm hug. "I'm glad you could make it."

"Like we would miss this," Stephen said. "My parents should be here soon too."

There had been a lot of changes in my life over the past few months. I'd moved in with Stephen right after we mated, and a few weeks later we got married, opting to have a small intimate ceremony in the clearing where we'd first met. Sometimes I missed living at Rosewater Manor, but I couldn't deny that I loved living with my mate.

Our lives had meshed together surprisingly well. His family had welcomed me into the fold wholeheartedly, and his parents had become good friends with my own parents. We'd even adopted a cat that had turned up in our yard one day. She was still a little nervous about Stephen, but she'd definitely warmed up to him. Life was good.

Stephen and I made our way over to where Cami and Meri were standing, watching the guests mingle.

"Hey girls, what's new?"

My sisters both greeted me with a hug. "I'm going to Denver for a Samhain retreat," Pepper told us, referring to the Wiccan holiday that coincided with Halloween. "I want to get in touch with my inner Goddess."

Meri rolled her eyes behind Pepper's back, but didn't say anything.

"That sounds fun," I said encouragingly. "I..."

I stopped as I saw Meri grab her head. "What is it, Meri? What do you see?"

"Whiteness falls from the sky," she gasped. Having a vision always made her head hurt.

"It's a little early for snow, Turmeric," Pepper teased.

Just then we heard a screech. We whirled around just in time to see two kids crash into the table where the cake was. Meri had insisted on getting my parents a ridiculously expensive wedding cake for their anniversary. They hit the table just at the right angle to make it tip forward. The cake flew up in the air before falling to the ground in a shower of white frosting.

"Whiteness falls from the sky all right," Stephen laughed.

I poked him in the side, and he pivoted to pull me into his arms. He pressed a kiss to the scar on my neck, the spot where he marked me as his mate. The spot throbbed beneath his lips. I pushed him a way with a laugh, but he looped his arms around me, holding me close.

"I love you, Chamomile."

I looked up into his eyes and saw the truth shining there. The bond between us was real, and it was its own kind of magic. "I love you too, Wolfie."

*** Keep reading for Meri's story, "Psychic Flashes" ***

Psychic Flashes

The Magical Midlife Series
By
Rose Bak

Copyright

About This Book

Her psychic skills must be on the fritz again...there's no way that she's about to fall in love with a wolf!

Meri's family has always been a little bit different. The daughter of a witch and a psychic, she frequently has visions of the future. Unfortunately, they're seldom very helpful. Want to know if something bad will happen tomorrow? Don't ask her. But if you're looking for your lost keys, Meri's your girl.

Most of her visions don't come true, so when she sees herself curled up with a hot older guy who likes to howl at the moon, she figures it's just another useless psychic flash.

Preston never asked to be a wolf shifter, but now that the billionaire CEO is stuck in the paranormal world, he figures he might as well learn how to make the best of it. He thinks he's adjusting well, until his wolf charges at a woman who he learns is his fated mate. She's nothing like the women he normally dates, but the curvy little psychic is about to turn his world upside down...

They say opposites attract, but can this unlikely pair really find true love?

Dedication

For everyone who believes in magic. I do too.

Meri

"Why do I let you talk me into this? I hate running."

I rolled my eyes at my melodramatic sister.

"Because you're thirty-five years old now Peppermint. You need to keep yourself healthy."

"I wouldn't need to run if I had a mate like Cami. I could be having hot monkey sex all day instead." She sighed loudly. "My Goddess, I'm so tired. How far have we gone?"

I glanced at my Garmin watch. "Just under a mile."

"I need to walk for a few minutes."

We slowed down just in time for the familiar feeling of a vise gripping my head in anticipation of a psychic flash. I stopped walking, holding my head between my hands as the vision came. It was me, sleeping, with a gray-muzzled wolf curled around me. The same wolf I'd been dreaming about for the past few weeks.

"What is it, Meri?" Pepper asked. "What do you see?"

I shook my head. "Nothing that makes sense."

That was true with about half of my visions. We came from a magical family. My mother was a strong witch, and my father was a well-known psychic. Unfortunately, their skills were diluted with their children. Our oldest sister Cami had some magic powers, but it was mostly things like starting fires and moving pencils. If she had to do something more complicated, she usually messed it up.

I'd inherited some of Dad's psychic powers. I had a vision at least once a day, and sometimes they were spot on. But often they either made no sense or they were something useless, like a vision of why the neighbor's cat was injured or a premonition about rain. If only I'd have a vision of the winning lottery numbers...

Poor Pepper had no powers at all. She was just a plain old human, and it bugged the hell out of her, as if being the middle sister wasn't hard enough.

69

"Come on Turmeric," Pepper said, calling me by my full name. "What was it?"

As if being the town weirdos wasn't enough, our parents had saddled us with ridiculous names. My oldest sister Cami's real name was Chamomile, Pepper's real name was Peppermint, and mine was Turmeric. Needless to say, I preferred to be called Meri.

"I saw an older wolf, sleeping next to me," I admitted, knowing exactly where Pepper's mind would go.

"Oh for Goddess sake, are you going to get a mate now too? What happened to that guy you saw with me? I'm destined to be alone, aren't I?"

Last year our oldest sister Cami had done a love spell to help Pepper find a mate. Right afterwards, I saw a vision of a wolf. It turned out to be Stephen, coming to find his fated mate. Unfortunately for Pepper, he was meant to be with Cami, not her. I'd later seen a vision of Pepper telling us that her mate was a monster, but that had never materialized.

Damn these glitchy skills of mine. I never knew what was real or not.

"It was just a flash Pepper. Like I've told you a hundred times, it could have meant anything, or nothing at all."

Unlike Cami and me, Pepper had been actively looking for a partner for several years, with no luck. Ever since she was a little girl, she'd dreamed about a wedding and having babies. As for me, I figured if it happened, it happened, and if not, it was clearly not meant to be.

"Come on, let's run."

We took off down the road again, each lost in our own thoughts. It was a cool morning, although it would likely be hot later, and I let myself enjoy the feeling of moving my body as we ran down the quiet country road.

A few minutes later we saw a giant dog come running towards us. As he got closer, I realized that it was a wolf. That wasn't too unusual around here; the neighboring town of Greysden had been founded by wolf shifters. The town had become a haven for shifters of all types who wanted to be free to explore their dual natures.

The wolf growled deeply, his eyes fixing on me as he barreled towards us. Pepper and I stopped running, not wanting to trigger his predator instinct, but he still kept coming towards me. Before I knew what was happening, the wolf leapt up on me, knocking me flat on my back on the side of the road. The animal stared down at me, blue eyes intense, paws on my shoulders, tongue hanging out in a canine smile.

"Hey, asshole, snap out of it and get off me!" I yelled. "You weigh a ton!"

The air shimmered, and the wolf was replaced with an incredibly handsome older man. He had dark hair with a few streaks of silver, a dark scruff, a strong square jaw, and those incredible blue eyes. He also was naked, and his rather large cock was hardening against my thigh.

"Mate!" he growled, his voice low and deep. "Mine!"

"Oh no," I mumbled. "Not this again."

Preston

I stared down at the freaked out face of the woman I'd attacked – well, my wolf had attacked – and wondered once again which god I'd pissed off.

Six months ago, I'd had a great life. As the billionaire heir to the Rutherford Industries fortune, I had a penthouse overlooking Central Park, a corner office with not one but two administrative assistants, and a collection of models and actresses on speed dial, each one willing to go out with me on a moment's notice. My life was orderly and predictable.

Until the night I was mugged. It had been an unseasonably warm night and I'd decided to walk home from the office. Without any warning, I'd been surrounded by a group of five men, and shoved into an alley.

I'd assumed they were just after my wallet, until one of the guys bit me. I'd been laying in an alley, holding onto the wound on my shoulder, wondering if I was going to die, when by some stroke of luck the cops had come by. My attackers scattered, and at the time I thought my biggest worry was an infection from the bite.

Turns out it was no ordinary bite. That became clear two weeks later when I started hearing a voice in my head. I thought maybe I was going crazy, but then I turned into a wolf. Seriously. One minute I was a man, the next minute I was all fur and fangs, racing through Central Park and scaring tourists who thought I was a rabid dog.

Even more shocking than turning into a wolf? Turning back into a man and finding myself naked in the park, with no clue where my clothes had gone or what had just happened.

That's when I learned that there was another world that existed side by side with the human world. I'd thought shifters were just something in movies, but I couldn't have been more wrong. As my senses

72

heightened, I became aware that I wasn't the only person who shared my body with an animal.

I wasn't really sure how to broach the topic of my change with someone, not wanting to sound like a lunatic. But as it happened, my friend and head of security, Duncan, recognized the change in me and came to my aid. He asked me if anything unusual had happened to me lately, and I told him the whole story about the guys in the alley and my new ability to grow fangs and a tail.

He told me all about the supernatural world, and I learned that the group who'd attacked me were something called rogues, the criminals of the shifter world. I still didn't know why they'd targeted me. Duncan thought maybe it was a gang initiation, or just some teens feeling their wild oats. Whatever their motivation, they'd violated shifter law.

Duncan took it upon himself to teach me about the supernatural world. He also tried to help me learn to control my shifts, something natural born shifters learned when they were very young.

It was a struggle. My wolf was very headstrong, and I had difficulty controlling him. He kept shifting at the most inopportune times, and I'd had several close calls around humans. Finally, Duncan suggested that I think of moving to a shifter area where I could learn more about my dual nature in a place where accidental shifts wouldn't raise eyebrows.

And so, the Greysden branch of Rutherford Industries was born. I'd purchased an old office building and completely remodeled it, building myself a luxury apartment on the top floor. My parents and most of my friends thought I'd lost my mind. They didn't understand why one of New York City's most renown playboys had moved to the backwoods of Colorado. It wasn't like I could tell them the truth. They'd have me locked up in the loony bin before I took a breath.

Since I'd moved here, things had been going pretty well. I'd learned how to run my empire from Greysden, and when I wasn't working,

Duncan and some new shifter friends in the area taught me about being a wolf.

What they hadn't taught me? What to do if my wolf tackled a young woman. A woman who felt delicious pressed against my naked body.

"Oh my God, I'm so sorry," I said, moving off the woman and offering her a hand.

Mine. Mine. Bite her. Mine. A voice was chanting non-stop in my head.

Ignoring my outstretched hand, the young woman got to her feet gracefully. Whoever this woman was, she was beautiful. Short and curvy, she had long straight hair that was darker on the top, blonde on the bottom. Her eyes were the deepest brown, and her lips...well, let's just say they made me think of very naughty things.

"I can't believe this is happening again."

The voice behind me startled me. All of my senses were so tuned to the woman I'd knocked over that I hadn't even noticed the other woman who was with her.

"It's not what you think it is, Pepper," the woman said. "He's obviously confused."

Suddenly the woman grabbed her head with one hand, my forearm with the other, grimacing in pain. Her eyes shot up to mine, wide and shocked.

"You were attacked by rogue wolves? That's terrible."

I frowned.

"How did you know that?" I asked in surprise. Duncan was the only person I'd told what happened.

"I'm kind of psychic," she replied.

I rolled my eyes. "Yeah, okay, sure. You're psychic. Well, sorry about running you over, crazy lady. If you're not hurt, I'll just be going now."

I took a deep breath and tried to call my wolf forth, but nothing happened. God, my inner animal was stubborn. It was like sharing my body with a toddler.

We must stay with our mate, the voice in my head admonished. My wolf, or so I was told by my new shifter friends.

I looked around to see both women were staring at my naked ass. I was glad I was so religious about my workout routine. I might be forty-five years old, but I wasn't going to let my body go to hell like so many guys my age. My ass was a work of art. And my lean body mass had only improved since I was turned into a shifter.

"Are you having problems shifting?" the alleged psychic asked sympathetically.

"He has performance issues," the other woman cackled.

"He's a new wolf, it's hard for him to manage his shifting yet," the girl I'd tackled explained to her companion.

I wasn't sure how she knew all that.

Our mate is smart as well as beautiful, the voice in my head said confidently. I had no clue what he was talking about.

Come on, wolf, we have work to do. We'll come back later.

To my shock, the next time I tried to bring on a shift, it worked. My wolf was pissed about leaving the woman, but at least it was learning who was boss.

With a quick glance over my shoulder, I ran back towards Greysden, my wolf whining in my head the entire way. I needed to talk to Duncan and figure out what had just happened before my wolf attacked someone else.

Meri

"Well, that was weird."

"Yeah. Let's head back, I need to get ready for work," I told my sister.

"Which job is this?" Pepper asked.

It was a fair question. I had a lot of jobs. I worked in the family bookstore once a week, did a couple shifts a week at a coffee shop in Greysden called Bearly Beans, did dog walking and in-home pet sitting, waitressed at banquets at the Greysden Hotel, and now I had the event planning business I'd started last year.

That was my real passion. I'd been planning parties for friends for years, but after a friend referred me to another friend who was planning an engagement party last year, I realized I could put my business degree to use and turn that into an actual business.

Given that we lived in a small town surrounded by other small towns, I'd been pleasantly surprised with how well the business was going. I'd been picking up events at the rate of about one per month, mostly parties for birthdays, engagements, and retirements. If my client list kept growing, I was confident I could turn event planning into a full-time business. I didn't need a lot of money, but I wanted to at least be comfortable, and maybe afford health insurance for the things I couldn't heal with herbs.

"It's a meeting for my event planning gig," I told Pepper. "I've been focusing on drumming up new business and getting more regular clients. What I really want to do is branch out to corporate clients, that's where the money is. I have a meeting at Rutherford Industries to talk about planning a company picnic for them this summer."

"Rutherford Industries? That huge company that relocated to Greysden from New York City?"

I nodded. "Yeah, if I can get this contract, I'm hoping I can become their regular event planner and line up some other corporate gigs. If

I can finally make the business profitable, I can cut back on my other jobs."

"Well, good luck little sister."

A few hours later I pulled my little electric car into the lot of Rutherford Industries. I'd toned down my usual eclectic wardrobe for this meeting, going with a relatively conservative green wrap dress and chunky heels. I'd pulled my hair back in a neat ponytail, and had limited myself to only two bracelets, one ring, and a rose quartz necklace.

Rutherford Industries was pretty fancy for these parts. It was the kind of place you'd find in Denver, not the mountains. They'd purchased an old factory and turned it into a sleek office space full of chrome, fancy office furniture, and rows and rows of boring grey cubicles. It made me itch, thinking about these poor workers trapped in this soulless office building forty hours a week.

I checked in with the receptionist, who looked like a Barbie doll but had the glimmer of an animal in her eyes. I wondered if the executives at Rutherford Industries knew that they'd moved into a town full of people who could turn into animals. Shifters were an open secret among humans, but most of them liked to pretend that shifters weren't real.

"Ms. Rosewater?"

I looked up as a curvy woman wearing a pencil skirt and jacket called my name. She was beautiful, with huge brown eyes and a fair complexion. I was pretty sure she was a human.

"Hi, yes, I'm Meri Rosewater."

"It's a pleasure to meet you. I'm Dianne, the administrative assistant for our company's CEO, Preston Rutherford the third."

Such a pompous sounding name, I thought with an internal eye roll as I followed her back to a conference room.

After refusing a beverage, I turned my attention to my proposal for a large corporate picnic in the Greysden town square which would be open to both the Denver and Greysden employees.

"We could have food carts, games, and play areas for the children," I explained as we went through my proposal. "The town of Greysden allows companies to rent out the park next the square, as long as regular residents aren't kept away."

"You think we should buy food for the entire town?" Dianne asked with a confused look.

I shook my head. "No, you'll give the employees and their families wrist bands that identify them as guests, and their meals and games will be charged to the company. Any other resident who wanders into the picnic area will pay with cash. I think it'll be great PR for the company and will also support the small businesses who partner with you."

"I agree. Thank you Meri, I can see you put a lot of work into this proposal, and I'll be sure to pass your recommendations on to Mr. Rutherford."

I was glad that Dianne seemed impressed by my presentation. After promising to let me know their decision within a few days, she walked me back out to the lobby.

"You! What are you doing here?"

I turned to see the guy from earlier, the wolf who couldn't control his shift. He was dressed now – such a pity – and wearing an expensive looking navy blue suit that looked like it was tailored to fit his tall frame. His hair was gelled back neatly, looking every bit the executive. I wondered what his role was here.

"Mr. Rutherford," Dianne responded. "This is Meri Rosewater, she's the event planner I told you about. She's got some great ideas for our company picnic this summer."

It figures. The guy who'd attacked me was the CEO here. I idly wondered if he'd moved here to be closer to other wolves now that he was a shifter. That would explain the decision to bring the company to this small town.

"A psychic event planner?" he asked sarcastically. "Isn't that something?"

My spine straightened and I met his skeptical gaze with a glare.

"Rosewater Events is the premiere event planning company in this area," I told him proudly. I didn't mention that I was the only event planning company in the area. "I come highly recommended."

"Do you have a lot of competition here in the middle of nowhere?" he asked sarcastically.

Goddess, what a jerk this guy was. I didn't need to be a psychic to figure out he wasn't going to give me this job. I turned to Dianne and gave her a professional smile.

"Please, feel free to check my references. They're included in the packet I gave you. Call me if you have any questions."

"Thanks for coming Meri, we'll—."

Dianne was interrupted by her boss. "We'll send you a psychic message if you're hired."

Dianne's mouth dropped open at his rudeness. I don't know what came over me, but I gave the man the finger. I'd never flipped anyone off in my life, but somehow it felt right.

"Since you're not psychic yourself, I'll use sign language to share my thoughts about your behavior, Mr. Rutherford." I sneered his name like it was a curse.

Dianne burst out laughing, but the woman at the reception desk gave me a glare. I wondered if the woman had a crush on her boss.

As I stalked out of the building, I told myself that if the people who worked at Rutherford Industries were that rude, I didn't want to work with them anyway. That didn't keep me from obsessing about those deep blue eyes the entire ride home.

Preston

"What's going on with you, boss?"

I looked up as Duncan strode into my office like he owned the place and dropped into a chair.

"Have a seat," I said drily.

Duncan and I had always had a strange relationship. I'd originally hired him because he wasn't an ass-kisser like most of the people I met. When the former Navy Seal told me off in his interview, I knew I could trust him to tell me the truth.

When I'd become infected with this werewolf virus, or whatever the hell it was that had turned me into a wolf shifter, and I learned he was a wolf too, he'd been a lifesaver. I now counted him as my closest friend.

"Dianne said you were really rude to some chick."

My wolf bristled inside me at the way he talked about Meri. The creature had been even more angry when I'd insulted her earlier. The damn thing had been clawing at my insides all afternoon, begging me to go find her and apologize. And bring her back to my apartment.

Our mate must come to our den, he'd told me about a dozen times today. *We must keep her close, away from other males.*

Duncan's head tilted, sensing my wolf's agitation.

"I ran into that woman earlier," I confided. "I was out for a run with my wolf and suddenly he just took over, running up this road and chanting 'mine, mine'. I didn't know what was going on. I couldn't control him. Then when we saw Meri running, he tackled her. He wanted me to bite her! I don't know what the hell was wrong with that damn wolf. I could barely hold him back."

"Ah," Duncan said enigmatically. "I see it's time for us to talk about mates."

"Mates?" I asked in confusion. "Like what they call friends in England?"

He shook his head.

"Every shifter has a fated mate, someone who is the other half of their soul. Most of the time we never find that person, but when we do, everything changes. We know the instant that we meet them that they're the one."

"The one what?"

"The one we're fated to spend the rest of our lives with. Our soulmate. It's like love at first sight, but way more intense."

That sounded right, but still I scoffed.

"That's ridiculous. It sounds like some fairy tale shifter moms tell their daughters."

"Look man, if I told you a year ago that people turned into wolves and other animals, what would you have said?"

"That you were crazy."

"Exactly. There's a lot about the shifter world you don't know yet, Preston. This is one of those things."

I studied him carefully, but I didn't detect a hint of guile in his expression.

"So, what? I'm supposed to believe that fate wants me to spend my life with some curvy little party planner who thinks she's a psychic?"

"Yep."

"Well, I refuse to accept that." I crossed my arms across my chest and leaned back in my chair. Even I could see I was being petulant.

"You can refuse to accept it all you want, but I can tell you right now, you're not going to be able to stay away from her until you mate her. It'll get harder and harder every day that you're apart. You might as well make it easier on yourself and accept your fate now."

"Are you saying if I sleep with her this feeling I have will go away?"

"Nope, the more time you spend with her, the more the mate bond will form between you. Soon you won't be able to resist biting her and tying your souls together for eternity."

"I guess I'd better stay away from her then."

Duncan stood up with a chuckle.

"Yeah, good luck with that, boss. Let me know when the wedding is so I can get my tux dry-cleaned."

Meri

"Turmeric? What's wrong?"

I looked up from my moping as my mother came into the library. The Rosewater Estate had been in our family for generations, and both Pepper and I still lived here with our parents. It wasn't as weird as it sounded. My parents spent half the year traveling, and both my sister and I had our own suites in the huge mansion we called home. Unlike a lot of families, everyone in my family actually liked each other.

We'd all been devastated when Cami had moved into her mate Stephen's house instead of moving him in here like we'd expected. Stupid wolf thought he'd have more privacy that way, even though he and Cami were here almost every day anyway.

"Nothing," I said glumly.

She gave me a look that had been making me spill my secrets since I was old enough to talk.

"I met this guy today, he's a wolf shifter. I think I might be his mate, but he's a total asshole."

"Are we talking about that wolf dude who doesn't know how to shift properly?" Pepper asked, entering the room and butting into the conversation. My sister was nosy as hell.

I nodded. "Yeah, it turns out he's Preston Rutherford, the CEO of Rutherford Industries. He tackled me earlier when Pepper and I were running and he growled 'mine', but then he ran off. I saw him again today at their company headquarters in Greysden, and he was super rude."

"Oh, I've heard of that guy," my mother said. She was pretty well connected in the supernatural world and usually had all the gossip.

"He was a normal," she explained, using the term shifters used for humans. "One night he was jumped by a group of rogue wolves in New York City, and one of them bit him and turned him against his will."

Usually shifters were made by being born to another shifter, but it was possible to turn a person later in life. It was strictly forbidden unless that human was their fated mate and gave explicit permission to be turned into a shifter. But just like in the human world, the shifter world had its fair share of criminals who enjoyed flaunting the rules.

"Hey Meri, your psychic skills were right about him being attacked by rogues," Pepper pointed out. "But what's he doing here?" she asked our mother.

"It's hard to learn to be a shifter once you're an adult, so he relocated to Greysden where he could be around other shifters and learn their ways."

"That's no excuse for being a jerk," I mumbled.

"Do you like him?" my mom asked curiously. "Is he attractive?"

"No way, he's totally old."

"He's forty-five," Pepper announced. "That's only eleven years older than you."

At my curious look she held up her phone.

"He's got his own Wikipedia page." She frowned. "This says he's a notorious playboy who's never had a long-term relationship in his life. Definitely not mate material."

"Once the mate bond is completed, it's biologically impossible for shifters to be attracted to another person," Mom reminded us.

"Whatever. I need to avoid him until it passes. He was making fun of my being a psychic, like he thought I was making it up or something."

"For a guy who can't control turning into a wolf, that's super rude," Pepper agreed loyally. "Besides, he doesn't know you well enough to make fun of your glitchy skills."

I stuck my tongue out at her. "Shut up, Peppermint Mugwort."

"Bite me, Turmeric Verbena."

"Girls," Mom chided. "Don't you think you're a little old for this?"

We both rolled our eyes.

***

Two days later I was working a shift at Cami's bookstore when my phone rang. Looking around to make sure there were no customers nearby needing help, I answered.

"Meri? Hi, this is Dianne from Rutherford Industries. We would love to offer you a contract for our company picnic if you're still interested in working with us."

"Really?" I asked in surprise. I'd figured flipping off their CEO had put me out of the running.

"Yes. We loved your proposal and we're willing to offer you a 50% premium on top of your very generous bid to ensure that everything is perfect."

"Does your boss know about this?" I asked curiously.

"Yes. Mr. Rutherford approved the contract with one stipulation."

She paused and I felt a whisper of unease. "He wants to work with you directly."

"I'm sorry?"

She cleared her throat. "Mr. Rutherford, um, likes to be involved in employee events."

It was painfully obvious that she was lying. I just didn't know what was actually going on.

"I'm going to email you the contract," Dianne continued. "Call me if you have questions, otherwise we'll look forward to hearing back from you soon. Assuming that you are still interested in working with us, we'd like to set up some planning meetings as soon as possible."

I was still staring into space when my sister returned, her husband Stephen at her side. She'd taken over Rosewater's Magical Emporium from our parents several years ago, putting her business degree to good use. Pepper and I were glad to let her buy our parents out; neither of us loved the store as much as Cami did, although I didn't mind picking up shifts to help out – and make some extra money.

"How's it going?" Cami asked.

I felt the telltale stabbing in my head and gripped the counter before turning my shocked eyes to my sister.

"Oh my Goddess, you're pregnant!"

Cami gasped. "How did you know? We just found out ourselves an hour ago."

I pointed at my head. "Psychic, remember? By the way, it's twins."

Stephen wrapped his arms around my sister's waist as her knees gave out.

"I wonder if they'll be witches or shifters?" she mused.

"Definitely shifters," Stephen said confidently.

"You wanna bet on that?" I asked.

He eyed me carefully. "No."

"Good plan."

Preston

I paced around my office waiting for Meri to get there for our first planning meeting for the company picnic. Maybe this was a bad idea spending time with her, but my damn wolf had been tearing me up inside ever since she walked out of here five days ago. I was hoping if we spent some time together, my wolf would see how unsuitable she was and get over his little crush on her.

Not a crush, my wolf growled. *She's our mate. We must claim her.*

When I'd first been changed, the wolf had mostly spoke to me in impressions and visuals that he somehow pushed into my mind. But ever since we'd jumped on Meri, he'd been communicating in English as well. Duncan had explained that it was pretty typical that once a wolf got more comfortable he'd begin to speak in words. Now I couldn't get the damn thing to shut up.

Mate! She's here! Let's go to our mate!

I looked out the door and sure enough, Dianne was leading Meri to the conference room. I grabbed a pad of paper and a pen like the grown-up executive I was, and headed in.

In contrast to the professional look that she'd sported last time she was here, today Meri was dressed in a long black skirt with some kind of ruffle at the bottom, black sandals laced over her ankles, and a white peasant shirt. Several beaded bracelets graced her wrists, and a long necklace with a black stone on it hung between her shapely breasts. Her multi-colored hair hung straight down past her shoulders.

I sniffed deeply, scenting the faint citrus smell that I now associated with Meri, feeling my cock twitch in my pants.

"Hello Meri, thanks for coming today."

She looked at me suspiciously. "Shall we get started?"

I had to admit that the young woman was organized. She'd come prepared with a timeline, a list of tasks, and some great ideas. I'd worked with several event planners over the years, and Meri was clearly very good at what she did. Plus, her references had been impeccable.

My wolf was quiet the entire meeting, happy to have his mate nearby.

When the hour was up, I was torn between wanting to keep her here and wanting her to go far away so I could concentrate on something else. Anything else. Like how she was probably too young for me. She looked like she was fresh out of college for cripe's sake.

"How old are you?" I asked abruptly.

Both Meri and Dianne gave me a look that conveyed that the question was inappropriate.

"I don't see how that's your business," Meri said primly. Her eyes flashed with irritation.

"I could probably google you and find out," I replied.

"Thirty-four," she bit out, leaping from her chair.

I raised my eyebrows in surprise. She was still eleven years younger than me, but there wasn't quite the age gap that I'd imagined there to be. Damn, there went one of my concerns about being with her.

"Dianne, I'll email you..."

She paused, her hand going to her head like she was in pain. Her eyes turned glassy.

"Are you okay, Meri?" Dianne asked.

"Your prescription sunglasses are stuck between the passenger seat and the center console, way at the bottom near the floor."

"What the hell are you talking about?" I asked.

She ignored me, her gaze on Dianne.

"Really? Oh my God Meri, thank you. I paid four hundred dollars for those, and I haven't been able to find them for weeks."

Meri gave her a warm smile that I wished was directed at me.

"Glad to help. I can show myself out. Goodbye."

She hustled out of the room, and I looked at my assistant in bemusement.

"Do you really think she's a psychic?" I asked.

"I don't know how she'd know about my lost sunglasses otherwise," Dianne responded. "Besides, there are a lot of different people in this world, Preston. I believe magic exists if you know where to look. You should know that even better than I do."

She gave me a look that made me wonder if she knew more about me than I thought she did. Dianne was one of the employees who'd followed me from New York, so it was likely that she'd seen the change in me after I'd gotten bit. I didn't think she was a shifter herself, but she seemed to know more than she was letting on, that's for sure.

"Your mate is beautiful," Duncan said, appearing in the doorway just as Dianne walked out. The guy had the most uncanny ability to fade into the woodwork like he was invisible.

Deep inside me, my wolf growled angrily. I bared my teeth and Duncan laughed.

"Settle down, buddy. I know she's yours."

"She's not mine," I said stubbornly. "She's too young and too weird. Totally not my type."

"I know you normally like those vapid and sophisticated women built like human clothes hangers, but your wolf knows your true desires. You just gotta learn to trust it."

He walked closer, clasping his hand on my shoulder.

"I know our world is new to you, but most shifters spend their whole lives hoping to find their true mate. If I were you, I'd ask myself why fate thinks she's a perfect match for you. And do it fast, before some human stakes his claim on your mate."

My wolf huffed in agreement.

The next day I was walking down the main street in Greysden when my wolf started freaking out.

Our mate! She's here. Our mate!

I followed my nose to Bearly Beans, the local coffee shop. I knew from previous visits that a bear shifter named Charlie ran the place.

Charlie greeted me by name, but I ignored him, looking around for my mate.

"What are you...? Oh wait, I know that look."

Just then Meri came out of the back, carrying a tray of muffins. I growled deep in my throat as she brushed against Charlie in the tight space. My fangs pressed against my lips as I tried to hold my wolf back from slicing the throat of the easy-going bear.

He's got a mate, I reminded my wolf. We'd met his human mate Theresa a couple of times while visiting the shop for a caffeine fix.

"What are you doing here, Meri?" I growled.

She jumped, almost dropping the tray of muffins.

"Oh. Preston. Hi. I'll be with you in a minute."

Charlie watched us in amusement. "You guys know each other?"

"She's my event planner," I bit out.

"Well, she's my barista," Charlie responded, his easy-going tone hardening. "So I'm going to need you to keep your wolf in check. Now please order something or move out of the way."

He nodded at the line forming behind me. I took a deep breath, willing my wolf to calm down. He was freaking out about all the other men in the shop being near our mate.

"Coffee, black. And one of those muffins."

Meri raised one eyebrow at my tone, so I added, "Please."

"You need to stop working here," I bit out as I handed Meri a twenty.

"You need to mind your own damn business," she responded. "Here's your change."

I shoved the change into the tip jar, still staring at her.

"Enjoy your coffee," she told me with forced sweetness. "Preferably somewhere else. Next!"

Meri

"Turmeric, someone's here for you."

I frowned as my mother's voice carried down the hallway. I wasn't expecting anyone. Walking down the long stairway from my suite on the second floor, my steps faltered as I noticed Preston standing at the bottom of the staircase with my mother. He was dressed like an ad for some rich guy cologne, with neatly pressed khakis, a white polo, and loafers. I resisted the urge to roll my eyes.

"Preston, what are you doing here?"

My mom looked between us curiously.

"Turmeric dear, why don't you invite your friend into the parlor, and I'll bring you some tea?"

It was easier to go along with her than argue, so I pointed towards the parlor.

"This way," I told Preston.

"Turmeric?" he asked as we walked up the hallway.

"My real name," I explained. "Don't ask."

We settled into chairs across from each other, and he looked around the room curiously. It hadn't changed much since my grandmother was alive. The shelves were filled with books, goddess statues, and various magical paraphernalia. The furniture was old but solid, and we kept the room spotlessly clean.

I'd seen him three times this week: once for our meeting at Rutherford Industries, and twice when he'd come into Bearly Beans. The second time he came in he'd settled himself into a chair and watched me work for over an hour, growling at any male who came close to me, until Charlie kicked him out. My boss was really easy-going, but he still was a predator, and he was not afraid to flex his bear muscles if the situation called for it.

"What are you doing here Preston?" I asked. "And how did you know where I live?"

91

"I, um...," he paused as my mother walked in with a steaming teapot and two cups. "Wow, that was fast."

"It's magic," my mom winked as she backed out of the room.

Preston looked confused.

"My mom's a witch," I explained. "It really is magic."

"Witches exist?" he asked dubiously.

"Most of the creatures you thought were fairy tales exist...shifters, witches, vampires, even psychics."

He had the good grace to look uncomfortable.

"I owe you an apology. Dianne found her glasses, and you knew about me being a new shifter, so clearly you have some, um, psychic abilities."

I nodded. "Okay, well thanks for stopping by."

"There's something else I want to talk to you about," he started.

We were interrupted by my two sisters rushing into the room as if they'd heard I was in here with a guy.

"Well, well, well, what's going on in here, Turmeric Verbena?"

I shot my sister a glare. "None of your damn business, Peppermint Mugwort."

Preston raised his eyebrows.

Pepper reached over to shake his hand, and I resisted the sudden urge to growl at her for touching my man. Wait, what?

"Hi, we didn't get a chance to introduce ourselves the other day. I'm Meri's sister Pepper, and this is our other sister, Chamomile Ginseng."

"Cami," my sister corrected.

We all hated our full names, which is why we regularly used them to torture each other.

"Our parents named us all after plants," I explained needlessly.

Preston bit his lip, clearly biting back a sarcastic reply. Not that I blamed him on this one.

"Do you guys mind? Preston and I are trying to talk." I looked pointedly at the door.

"It's our parlor too," Pepper pointed out.

"You all live here?" Preston asked.

"I live with my husband in Greysden," Cami corrected. "He's a wolf shifter, like you."

"And are you a psychic too?" he asked her.

She laughed. "Goddess no, I'm a witch, like our mother."

"Except our mother's witchcraft actually works," Pepper interjected.

"At least I have some powers," Cami retorted. "It's better than being a boring old human like *some* people."

"Get out!" I yelled at my sisters.

"Are you okay?" Pepper mouthed, nodding towards Preston.

That was the thing about my sisters: we antagonized each other mercilessly, but if someone bothered one of us, they'd feel the full wrath of the sisterhood.

I nodded. "I'm fine."

As soon as they were gone, I turned back to Preston. He was staring at me like I was some puzzle he needed to work out.

"What did you want to talk about?" I finally asked when he remained silent.

"You're totally not my type, and clearly you and your family are...different from what I'm used to," he started, his voice formal and stilted. "But I'm still drawn to you for some reason. I would like to go out with you on a date. Well, my wolf wants me to go out with you anyway."

I couldn't decide if I was hurt or angry. I decided to go with angry.

"Well, as flattering as that invitation is, I'll have to decline. Thanks for stopping by."

He looked stunned. "But...I'm one of New York's most eligible bachelors."

"Bully for you. Too bad this is Colorado. Bye now."

I got up and gestured for him to follow me. He still had this look of stunned confusion on his face when I pushed him out the door and slammed the door behind me.

Preston

I spent the next few days in a foul mood. Even Dianne was avoiding me, mostly communicating with me through email even though her desk was right outside my office door.

Duncan finally came to my office at the end of the day.

"How about we take our wolves out into the woods for a run?" he suggested. "Based on the way you've been acting, I'm betting your wolf is pretty riled up."

I felt a twinge of guilt. I might be the CEO, but I'd never been the kind of guy who was rude to his staff.

"Yeah, that would be great. I can't trust him not to take over and run to Meri's house, so it would be good to have another wolf with me."

"What's eating you, man? You've been pissing people off all week."

As we walked the few blocks to the woods that surrounded Greysden I told him about my visit to the Rosewater home, omitting the fact that I'd asked Meri out and been shot down.

"The place was totally weird, and her family seems...well, not normal. Meri didn't seem too happy to see me either. I think she hates me."

"Look Preston, you're in Colorado now. People here are quirky, and that's just the regular humans. You weren't happy in New York..."

"My wolf wasn't happy," I corrected.

"Really? Because I've known you for a long time, and you never seemed particularly happy fighting traffic, making your way through models, and attending boring galas. You've seemed much more relaxed here."

It was true.

"Mate issue aside, if you want to make friends here in Greysden, you're going to have to get that stick out of your ass and stop being such a snob. These people aren't less than you just because they dress

95

differently or don't have a stock portfolio the size of a small country's economy. You need to loosen up, man."

"Yeah, you're right," I admitted. "The longer I'm here, the more I see how fake all those people were in my old life. But...I just don't know how to approach Meri. It feels like every time I see her I just make her hate me more, but it's getting harder to stay away."

We reached a clearing a short distance into the woods and took off our clothes, tucking them beneath a bush. That was the nice thing about living in a shifter town, there were lots of places to run in your animal form, and no one stole from you when you left your belongings behind.

I took a deep breath and exhaled slowly, calling forth my wolf. I felt a flash of intense pain as my bones broke and re-set and my muscles lengthened. Fur sprouted from my pores, as my tail, fangs, and claws extended. Everything seemed so much simpler when I was in my animal form. I inhaled with an open mouth, taking in the now-familiar scents of woods and animals.

Duncan took off and I followed him, enjoying the feeling of my paws hitting the soft-packed ground. All of my senses were heightened in this form, and I felt connected to nature in a way I'd never been when I was fully human.

We'd been running hard for about an hour when I smelled it: the distinct scent of my mate. With a yip I took off towards the scent, Duncan's wolf following me.

What's happening? he asked me telepathically.

Mate! Mate!

Before he could respond, we came to a clearing where Meri was gathering plants into a large basket. Meri turned as we approached, her hands full of leaves. She looked as surprised to see me as I was to see her.

She was wearing loose shorts, a fitted tee shirt that hugged her luscious curves, and battered running shoes. Her hair was up in one of those messy buns that women liked, and her face was completely bare of make-up. She looked stunning.

"Preston?"

My wolf preened that she recognized us in this form. I skidded to a stop in front of her and pressed my large wolf body against her legs. She giggled, leaning down to pet me, rubbing her small hand over my head and making my wolf grumble happily.

"You're so much less annoying as a wolf."

I inhaled her sweet citrusy scent and wondered why I thought it was a bad idea to be with her. Despite all of our differences, when she touched me, everything else faded away.

Leave us now, I told Duncan through our link.

Are you sure? You said you wanted to stay away from her.

I growled and he gave a little shake of his head before turning and running off through the trees, leaving me alone with my mate. I swear I could hear the asshole laughing in my mind.

Good luck.

Meri

"What are you doing here?" I asked the wolf in front of me.

I'd been thinking about Preston non-stop, despite my irritation with how he'd basically given me the Mr. Darcy routine in his ridiculous attempt to ask me out. My parents had raised me to know my own value, and there was no way I was going to settle for someone who seemed to like me against their will.

Preston's wolf pressed against me again and I giggled at the feeling of his fur rubbing against the skin of my bare legs. I ran my fingers over the soft fur between his ears, crooning, "Who's a good boy? Who's a good wolfie?"

The air shimmered and I heard a few pops before the wolf was replaced by a naked Preston, crouched on hands and knees. He rose to his feet, apparently unconcerned about his nakedness.

"Why are you out here alone?" he demanded. "The woods are dangerous."

I rolled my eyes, something I seemed to do a lot around him. This guy had a lot of nerve, trying to tell me what to do. We weren't even friends, let alone anything more.

"I grew up in these woods. I know them way better than you do."

I stepped away and resumed my hunt for the medicinal plants my mother asked me to gather for her. Finding something she needed, I squatted down to pick a few leaves. I could sense Preston standing where I'd left him, watching me. I looked at him over my shoulder, noticing his gaze was fixed firmly on my ass.

"Is there something you need?"

He flushed as he raised his eyes. "I can't get you out of my mind," he finally said.

I stood up and turned to face him, keeping my eyes fixed to his face and resisting the temptation to check out his chiseled body.

"That sounds like a personal problem."

Usually I was the gentle sister, but I was still smarting from his harsh words the other day. I didn't want to admit that I was having the same problem. Preston had been on my mind almost constantly since the day I met him, and it had only gotten worse the more time I spent with him. It was really starting to piss me off.

He stared at me intently as he took several steps towards me, like an animal stalking its prey.

We both jumped at the unexpected crack of thunder in the distance. The sky opened, and suddenly it was pouring rain. Preston continued his deliberate approach, and I used every bit of willpower I had to not retreat.

When he was only an inch away from me he stopped, his eyes searching mine. The warm rain had already drenched us, and small droplets ran down his face. He growled deep in his throat and without another word, he lowered his lips to mine.

This wasn't the gentle and tentative first kiss that I'd shared with so many other guys. No, this kiss was immediately hard and rough, almost feral. He nipped sharply at my lower lip, demanding entrance, and I opened with a gasp. His tongue swooped in, exploring and dominating my mouth.

My entire body lit up, like hitting the switch on a string of Christmas tree lights. I groaned against his mouth, lifting my hands to run my fingers through the wet strands of his dark hair.

I felt my back press against the bark of a tree and realized dimly that I hadn't even been aware that we'd been moving. He ran his large hands down my hips, circling the back of my legs and lifting me up, trapping me between the tree and his hard body. Instinctively, I wrapped my legs around his waist and rolled my hips against his, looking for the pressure I needed. I could feel the hardness of his growing erection against my center as the kiss went on and on.

Preston broke away, panting heavily, and stared into my eyes, the flicker of his wolf visible in the dark depths. Rain drops stuck to his long eyelashes, way too long for a man.

"I need you, Meri. So much." His voice was more wolf than human.

When I didn't reply, he released my legs, setting my feet back on the ground.

"Take off your shirt," he rasped.

"Was there a please in there somewhere?" I sassed.

He reached forward, claws extended, and I pulled off my t-shirt before he shredded it. It had a beautiful illustration of Gaia on it and there was no way I wanted it ruined. Tossing it to the side, I reached behind me to unclasp my bra, sending it flying. My heavy breasts bounced as they were released.

He gave me a look that was full of appreciation and heat, and dropped to his knees, large hands circling my waist.

"Beautiful," he breathed.

His lips wrapped around one nipple, sucking it into the moist heat of his mouth. I gripped his shoulders tightly as he circled and teased the nub into a hard peak, then gave the other one the same attention.

I swear I was close to coming just from the nipple stimulation. Somewhere in the back of my mind, I knew I was annoyed with him, I just couldn't remember why.

Preston slid my shorts down my legs, followed by my panties, and lifted one foot at a time as he drew my clothing off. I stood completely naked in front of him and tried not to be self-conscious about the soft swell of my belly and the thickness of my thighs. I was a curvy girl, my body softly rounded, and I knew that I wasn't everyone's cup of tea. Preston seemed to like my body though, judging by the almost reverent look he was giving me.

He extended his tongue and slid it between my folds, causing me to cry out in pleasure.

"You like that, do you?" he whispered before repeating the action again and again.

I made a sound of assent, unable to form any actual words at the moment. When I was a writhing mess, legs quaking, two seconds away from coming, I pulled on his hair.

"Inside me. Now," I ordered.

Preston's eyes widened and then he moved more quickly than I could have imagined as he leapt back up to his feet, lifted my legs around his waist, and shoved into me in one long thrust.

I screamed at the intrusion, my pussy clamping down tight. I'd never been with a man who wasn't wearing a condom, and it felt so different. Fortunately, I had an IUD so I could just enjoy the incredible sensation of him pounding into me.

"Fuuuck," I moaned, willing my muscles to relax.

Preston started moving, slowly at first, then picked up speed until he was banging me roughly against the tree. I couldn't do anything but hold on. It only took a few minutes before I was coming harder than I'd ever come in my life.

I bucked against him, my entire body shaking, and Preston pushed against me harder, holding me in place with his big body. I lowered my head, gripping the top of his shoulder with my teeth. The bite of pain triggered his own orgasm, and Preston gritted out my name before filling me with his warm seed.

He sagged against me, his face buried in my neck, as we both waited for our heartrates to slow again.

"Jesus Christ," he finally spoke. "What was that?"

His words broke the spell. I unwrapped my legs, lowering myself to the ground, and gently pushed on his chest until he stepped back. I had the sudden urge to get the hell out of there.

What had I done? Good Goddess, I'd just let a man who didn't even like me fuck me bareback against a tree. What was I thinking? This was not normal behavior for me.

"I don't know what that was," I answered, looking around frantically for my belongings.

He stood there looking shocked and confused while I grabbed my sodden clothes. Throwing my underwear and bra into my basket – they were way too wet to get on easily—I quickly pulled on my shorts and shirt.

"Well, thanks for the orgasm, Preston. Bye."

I ran away like I was being chased, only breathing again when I realized that he wasn't following.

Preston

I'd had sex with a lot of women in my time, and never once had a woman run away from me after sex. Usually, I had to kick them out, but not Meri – as soon as we were finished she had taken off like her feet were on fire.

It was a bit disconcerting. I mean, it had been the best sex of my life, and I had a lot of experience to compare it to. Maybe it wasn't as good for her though? She'd seemed to enjoy it. I was pretty sure she hadn't been faking that orgasm.

I stilled as I realized that we hadn't used a condom. I'd never forgotten a condom, even when I was a teen. My parents had drilled it into me from a young age that women would try to trap me by getting pregnant, eager to get their hands on my fortune. I had a vision of Meri rounded with my child, and I was surprised by how appealing it was. I knew instinctively that my mate was no gold digger.

The sky was still dumping buckets of rain, so I switched back to my wolf form and ran back through the woods towards Greysden. My wolf was pushing me to go after our mate, but I held it back through sheer will. I needed time to think, to process what had just happened.

Mate. Mate. You should have marked our mate so other men would know she is ours. She must come to our den now.

I ignored the wolf's whining. I needed to talk to Duncan, he'd know what to do. I ran towards his house on the edge of town and found him sitting on his back porch, watching the end of the rain.

"Hey there, I was wondering if you'd show up. How'd it go with your mate?"

I switched back into my skin and plopped my naked ass into a chair. "I'm so confused."

"What's confusing?" Duncan asked, reaching into a cooler next to his chair and handing me a beer. "You: wolf. Her: mate. You just need to claim her and live happily ever after. Your wolf knows what to do, man."

I felt a flush rise up my face. Duncan's eyes narrowed as he studied me.

"What?"

"We, um, well, you know...but when it was over, she ran away."

Duncan chuckled. "I thought you'd be better at that after all the women you banged in New York City."

"It was good. Great actually," I said defensively. "I mean, she seemed to enjoy it too. But then after, well, I'm not sure what happened."

"Look, I know this is hard for someone like you to believe, but a lot of women prefer to be wooed. She probably wants to know that she means more to you than just a quick screw in the woods."

My wolf growled at his casual dismissal of what had happened.

"This girl clearly doesn't care about your money and your power. You've got to romance her. Maybe try asking her on a date."

I felt my face flush even deeper, and I avoided my friend's eyes.

"I didn't tell you this earlier, but I asked her out on a date a few days ago when I went to her house. She told me no. I think I offended her somehow with the invitation."

He frowned. "What did you say exactly?"

"I simply told her that even though she isn't my normal type, and we have nothing in common, my wolf still wanted her."

"Jesus Christ, how can you possibly be this clueless?"

"What?" I asked defensively.

He took out his phone. "I'm going to text you a list of movies to watch. Don't do anything with this girl until you watch them. After you're done, we'll talk."

I spent the next couple of days watching what could only be described as "chick flicks". It was during "Pride and Prejudice" that I realized what I'd done wrong when I asked Meri out. Armed with my new understanding of women who weren't the same as the vapid models who'd chased me all my life, I decided to try again.

Meri's mother opened the door.

"You're here for Turmeric again?" she asked, looking amused. I wondered how much she knew about what had happened between me and her daughter.

"Yes ma'am," I said politely.

"She's working at the store."

"The coffee shop?" I asked.

"No, the bookstore."

"Wait. She works as an event planner, a barista, and she has a job at a bookstore?" I asked in confusion.

"Our Meri likes to stay busy," she explained. "She has a lot of jobs, those are just three of them. But today's she's doing a shift at our family store to help Cami out."

Seeing my blank expression she added, "Rosewater's Magical Emporium. It's on Main Street."

"Thank you."

As I headed back towards town, I resolved to talk to Meri about working so many jobs. That couldn't be healthy, and my wolf was worried. Well, honestly, so was I. Was she hard up for money or something? Her family lived in a mansion, and they owned a business, but maybe they were land rich and cash poor.

We must provide for our mate, my wolf reminded me.

Rosewater's Magic Emporium was like something out of that show about the teenage vampire slayer. It was an enormous space with shelves full of old books, crystal balls, amulets, statues, and an entire wall of dried herbs in jars. Literally half of the things in the store I couldn't identify.

"May I help...oh, it's you!"

Meri came around the corner with a look on her face that was less than welcoming. She was wearing a short black dress decorated with stars and moons. The dress hit her mid-thigh, baring her shapely legs down to the red cowboy boots that came up a few inches past her ankles. She had her long hair in some kind of complicated braid that ran across the top of her head, rings on every finger, and a row of beaded bracelets running up her arm. She looked funky and unique, like a hipster witch. She was stunning.

"What are you doing here, Preston? I assume you're not looking for crystals or a mortar and pestle?"

"Since I have no idea what a mortar and pestle is, I'm going to go with no."

I stuck my hands in my pockets, suddenly nervous.

"How have you been?"

She tilted her head and frowned.

"I'm working Preston. I have no time for small talk, so spit it out. Why are you here?"

"I feel like you don't like me very much."

"Yeah, you got that right," she said sarcastically. "Anything else we need to settle?"

"I'm sorry about what happened. In the woods I mean. I usually have a little more finesse. And I didn't even think about using a condom."

She looked around frantically. "We can't talk about that here. The walls have ears."

I wondered if she meant literally. Even as a baby wolf, I could feel the thrum of magic running through this store.

"Can I take you out to dinner tonight?"

She shook her head before I finished my question. "I'm working until nine o'clock."

"Tomorrow then?"

She stepped closer and I smelled the citrus scent that I associated with her. My wolf rolled around in my mind, thrilled to be close to his mate.

"Look, Preston…"

"Please," I interrupted. "One dinner, and if you still don't want to be around me I'll leave you alone."

"I thought your wolf thinks I'm his mate?"

"Yes," I confirmed.

"Will you be able to stay away if I tell you to?"

"Sure," I said cockily. "I'm in control, not my wolf."

I flinched as my wolf scratched at me from the inside, clearly disagreeing. Meri's eyes twinkled in amusement like she knew full well what was happening, but she didn't call me on it.

"Fine. One dinner, and then you leave me alone."

My wolf and I both sagged in relief.

"Awesome. I'll pick you up tomorrow at six."

Meri

When Preston came to pick me up, I was waiting on the porch, trying to avoid prying eyes. I was thirty-four years old and still my family was acting like this was my first date. Nosy assholes. Even Cami and Stephen were hanging out, trying to get a glimpse of what my mother called my "new beau."

I slid into Preston's car the minute it pulled to a stop in the driveway. It was some fancy foreign model, what a shock. Not. The car was fussy and pretentious, just like its owner. I wondered again why I'd agreed to this.

Because you're hoping for more orgasms, my conscience reminded me.

I still wasn't sure what had happened when I ran into Preston in the woods. One minute he was rubbing against my legs in his wolf form, the next minute he was pounding me into a tree. It had easily been the hottest experience of my life. I'd come so hard I could still feel it.

But then the orgasm haze had faded, and I remembered that he was some snobby rich guy who didn't like me too much. A guy who dated tall skinny models who were barely legal and probably ordered three leaves of lettuce when he took them to dinner.

If only I could keep the orgasm part and not have to deal with the snobby and irritating personality...

"Where are we going?" I asked.

"I thought we'd drive into Denver," he said. "I got us reservations at La Petite Rouge."

I huffed in annoyance.

"Look Richie Rich, I'm not dressed for some fancy schmancy place. I need to go somewhere where dinner is more than two bites of food arranged artfully on china."

"Do you have something better in mind?" he asked mildly.

I pointed to Main Street. "Go that way."

I directed Preston to the highway, heading away from Denver. After ten minutes of driving, we reached a small town that had some of the best food in Colorado.

"Pull off here," I directed. We drove through the small downtown area, which was very similar to Greysden, and ended up near a battered dock. My favorite taco cart was set up next to the lake, surrounded by picnic tables. A hand painted sign on the side of the cart read "Cortez Tacos". Christmas lights were strung between the cart and the nearby power poles, ready to be illuminated when it got dark out.

"We're eating here?" Preston asked dubiously as we exited the car.

"Trust me." I threaded my fingers through his and pulled him towards the long line of people waiting for their food. The Cortez Tacos cart was legendary in these parts.

I was wearing a little skater dress – my go-to during the summer. This one was a deep purple with geometric shapes in shades of red and blue. I'd paired it with my red cowboy boots and several pieces of jewelry made out of beads and crystals. I'd straightened my hair, leaving it long over my shoulders.

Meanwhile Preston was wearing navy blue dress pants with a pristine white button-up with only one button open. He was freshly shaved, and his hair was gelled back. Impishly I reached up and flicked open another button on his shirt. He gave me a curious look but didn't comment.

Standing there holding hands with him felt kind of nice, at least until he opened his mouth.

"Docs this place have to pass the health department inspection?" he asked suspiciously.

"Chillax, I would never steer you wrong on something as important as food."

We got to the front of the line, and I saw my friend Gabriel was working. A good friend from high school, he and four of his brothers owned the cart.

"Turmeric Rosewater, you little slut," he called out jokingly. "Where have you been?"

He raced out of the cart, pulling me away from Preston and engulfing me in a big hug that lifted my feet off the ground.

"Put me down, you big oaf," I laughed, smacking his shoulder. I heard a low growl behind me that I was certain came from my date.

"Gabriel, this is Preston. Preston, my good friend Gabriel."

The men shook hands, looking suspiciously at each other.

"What'll you have, baby? The usual?" Gabriel asked.

"Yeah and make it two. Plus two bottles of beer please."

Preston held out his credit card to pay, and I couldn't help but notice it was one of those fancy black ones. I pushed his hand away.

"It's cash only here."

He looked uncomfortable. "I don't carry cash."

I was already pulling my wallet out. "Don't worry, I gotcha."

"But..."

I gave him a frown. "Preston, no one will question your manhood if you let a girl buy you some tacos."

"Some tacos?" Gabriel said in mock outrage. "I think you mean the best damn tacos in Colorado."

I laughed. "My apologies. I stand corrected."

A few minutes later Gabriel handed us a tray and we headed over to one of the picnic tables. I handed Preston his plate and he looked confused.

"I thought you ordered tacos. Did we get the wrong order? These look like open-faced mini burritos."

"Those are tacos."

"Where's the hard shell?" he asked suspiciously.

"This isn't Taco Bell. These are freshly made Mexican street tacos, totally authentic. Eat up."

I folded the soft tortilla in half as Preston watched me intently. My eyes closed in pleasure as I tasted the seared carnitas mixed with vegetables and fresh cilantro. Preston folded his own taco carefully. He brought it to his lips slowly as if afraid this was all a prank, but his face softened in pleasure when he took his first bite.

"Holy crap Meri, these are fantastic."

"Told ya," I said, pointing my beer bottle at him. It was icy cold, just like I liked it. "You're in Colorado now, it's time to expand your culinary horizons."

"I guess it is."

He picked up his next taco, and the tortilla broke apart, sending a trail of taco innards down his white shirt. I laughed at his obvious mortification.

"That means you're going to have a lucky night."

Preston

I stared down in horror at the mess on my shirt. I looked around furtively to see if anyone was taking a picture of me, but no one was paying any attention to what was happening at our table. Back in New York, a Rutherford wouldn't dare let themselves be seen in stained clothing. I could just imagine my mother's face if she saw me now...

"That means you're going to have a lucky night," Meri said solemnly, drawing my attention back to the present.

I picked up a napkin and tried to clean the shirt, but it just made it worse.

"I guess this shirt is ruined," I said glumly.

"It's carnitas and vegetables. You just need to wipe it with the stain remover and run it through the washer when you get home. It'll be good as new."

I must've had a confused expression on my face because Meri shot me a surprised look.

"You do know how to use the washing machine, right?"

"Um. I have a cleaning lady who does the laundry."

She rolled her eyes. "Of course you do."

It was so interesting to be with someone whose values were so different than mine. It had literally never occurred to me to learn how to use the washing machine. There were always household staff around to take care of those kinds of things. With Meri, it was clearly some kind of moral failing to not do my own housework.

Someone brushed by the table, bumping Meri's shoulder. She moaned and gripped her head, which I was coming to recognize meant she was having a psychic vision.

"What?"

She was silent for a moment, her eyes unfocused. Suddenly she yelled, "Hey. Jake!"

The person who had just walked by turned back to us.

"Yeah? Do I know you?"

Meri shook her head. "No, but that girl you met at the club in Denver, Amy? She lost your number so she's going to the club tonight hoping to run into you again."

"Really?" he asked in obvious excitement. "She promised to call me and never did. I figured she was just blowing me off, especially since she never gave me her number in return."

"Nope, she wants to see you again. You should head over there though and catch her before she leaves. But don't take the Valley Highway, there's going to be a wreck that'll back up traffic for hours."

"Wow, thanks."

The young man raced off, a big goofy smile on his face. Meri picked up her last taco, attacking it with gusto. I tried not to stare at her. I couldn't imagine any of the women I'd dated eating so many tacos. Well, or any tacos. They were all skin and bones, talking incessantly about their fad diets. I'd literally never seen a woman who enjoyed food like Meri. It was a nice change, I realized.

A band started playing nearby, and Meri popped up out of her seat like a jack-in-the-box, grabbing our now-empty tray.

"Let's dance!"

We tossed our trash in the garbage can and she pulled me by the hand towards the large grassy area near the band. People were already starting to dance to the up-tempo beat. I'd taken dance classes as a boy, like everyone in my social group, learning the waltz and other ballroom dances. But I'd never danced to music like this. And I'd never seen anyone dance like Meri.

She raised her hands over her head, her entire body moving to the beat of the Mexican pop music the band was playing. I stood next to her, awkwardly shuffling, until she placed her tiny hands on my hips and moved them from side to side.

Drifting closer, she rose up on her toes, bringing her head closer to mine, and whispered, "Just close your eyes and feel the music, Preston. Your body knows what to do."

Wrapping my arms around her waist, I did just that. I closed my eyes, letting the music flow around me, and just moved. It was free and sensual, and all of my senses were heightened being this close to my mate.

My wolf loved having Meri in my arms as much as I did. Only a few inches separated us, and every time she shifted I could feel the air move around her. My cock hardened, pressing almost painfully against the zipper of my trousers.

I couldn't say how long we danced, but by the time we walked away from the make-shift dance area, I was sweaty and pleasantly tired. Meri's face was flushed, the hair at her temples damp.

"Let's go home and get you out of that shirt."

Oh crap, I'd totally forgotten about the large stain running down the front of my shirt. Meri had a way of making me forget everything except her.

We walked back to my car in silence. I automatically drove to my place on top of my office building, my wolf encouraging me to bring her back to our den. As I pulled into the garage on the first floor, Meri looked around.

"Wait. You live in your office building?"

"Yeah, I turned the top floor into an apartment. It's very convenient."

"It's very sad," she corrected. "There's more to life than work."

I was beginning to see that was true.

We headed for the elevator, and I scanned my keycard, sending the box up towards the top level. The air between us was charged, and with my newly discovered wolf senses, I could smell her arousal. That was handy. There was no doubt she wanted me as much as I wanted her.

I moved to pull her into my arms, but she pressed her palms against my chest. "Wait."

The elevator opened into my foyer, and Meri looked around curiously. My place was essentially a converted loft, with concrete walls and exposed beams. My designer had painted the walls a soft white, adding strategically placed abstract artwork in big, expensive frames. The furniture was Danish in style, with white upholstery and black metal frames. White area rugs tied the look together.

"Wow, this is a whole lot of white."

Meri did not sound impressed. My wolf felt disappointed that she didn't like our "den" as he called it.

"Where's the washing machine?"

I led her into the laundry room and unbuttoned my shirt, handing it to her.

"No way, rich boy. I'm not the hired help. You're going to do this yourself."

When I just stared at her she sighed.

"Lay the shirt flat over the top of the washing machine." At my blank look she added, "It's the one with the lid on top."

She reached up for something on the shelf next to the machines, and the hem of her dress lifted, giving me a tantalizing view of her muscular thighs.

"Here's the stain treatment." She pointed towards the taco stains with a small bottle that was oddly shaped. "You just blot the solution on top and around the stain until it's soaked through."

I pressed the bottle against the fabric and when nothing happened she added, "You have to take the cap off first, doofus. Jeez, do you really run an entire company?"

I flushed as I followed her instructions on how to apply the stain remover and rub it into the fabric. When she deemed it ready, she showed me how to add detergent and program the washing machine. I turned it on with the most ridiculous feeling of accomplishment.

"Now what?" I asked.

"We wait for the buzzer to go off, then we put it in the dryer."

"What should we do while we're waiting?"

She looked up at me from beneath her lashes.

"How about you show me your bedroom?"

My eyes widened. "Really?"

"Just keep your fangs to yourself."

Meri

Four weeks later...

The past month had flown by. I would have never believed it, but I was having fun with Preston. He'd started feeling more comfortable in his skin – as well as his fur – and with that he'd mostly lost the stick up his ass.

He was practically living in my suite at the Rosewater estate. After the first time we'd stayed over at my place, he'd declared that he felt more comfortable there than he ever had in his fancy penthouses. Not that I blamed him; I felt the same way.

It helped that my mom was in town and kept making him waffles for breakfast. I'd never seen a grown man so obsessed with waffles. If he stuck around, he was going to be sad the next time my parents left on one of their trips; they were often gone for months at a time.

Preston and my dad had bonded over baseball, although Preston was a Yankees fan while my entire family were loyal Rockies fans. After all these weeks together, Preston pretty much felt like a part of the family. I tried not to think too hard about how comfortable we were getting, just in case it didn't last.

Otherwise, we'd fallen into a routine. I continued to work at my various jobs, and as the CEO of Rutherford Industries, Preston also put in long hours at work. But every night we had dinner together, either at home or at some hole-in-the-wall place that I liked, and then we'd retire to my suite. Preston would play my body like an instrument and a couple of orgasms later we would fall into a deep sleep.

Waking up in Preston's arms had become my favorite part of the day.

The more time we spent together, the more relaxed and likable he became. He was learning to live like a regular person. I'd even gotten him wearing jeans and shorts. The first time I took Preston to Target, he'd been like a kid in a candy store.

"Everything's so cheap here!" he'd gushed. *"But it's still pretty nice."*

"Welcome to the middle class," I'd teased him. *"We hope you'll like our pizza."*

Meanwhile, Dianne and Preston and I were finishing up plans for the company picnic. It was still much more upscale than your average company picnic, but I'd convinced Preston to add carnival games and contests, like the three-legged race. We were expecting good attendance, with employees from the Denver branch joining those who worked at the Greysden office.

The day of the picnic dawned warm and sunny, a perfect end-of-the-summer day. I was attending both as the event planner and Preston's date, and I decided to wear this adorable little denim romper I'd purchased last summer and never wore. The shorts were short, the waist was fitted, and the neckline was low. With my curves, I looked like one of those 1940s pin-up girls, so I decided to go with the look, adding chunky red vintage sandals I'd found in my mother's closet. I was pretty sure they'd been my grandmother's. Us Rosewaters never threw anything out.

Pepper helped me pull my hair up into one of those complicated "Victory roll" designs they'd worn in the nineteen forties, with a red scarf folded up around my head like a headband, tied at the top. I'd added dark eye make-up, several coats of mascara, and bright red lipstick.

I loved the look and so did Preston. His fangs had dropped the minute he saw me.

That was the one point of contention between us. Preston and his wolf were both pushing for Preston to mark me and seal the mate bond, but something was holding me back. I didn't quite feel ready for the shifter equivalent of marriage, especially after knowing each other for only six weeks. My sisters both thought I was crazy, but I figured when the time was right, I'd let Preston bite me. Maybe.

The picnic was being held in the center of Greysden. We'd rented out the large park area across from Main Street, setting up the games on one side and a series of food trucks on the other. I'd even convinced Gabriel to bring the taco cart to the event. It was a great way for Rutherford Industries to offer a variety of food to the guests while supporting local small businesses.

Preston looked handsome in his newly purchased tan cargo shorts, a tight navy t-shirt with the Rosewater's Magical Emporium logo on it, and a pair of Nikes. He'd let his hair grow a little longer and it was tousled from the light breeze. He'd never looked hotter.

Well, he'd never looked hotter when he wasn't inside me. Another thing that had been great the last month: our sex life. We'd had sex at least once a day, usually twice, on just about every surface in my suite as well as his apartment. And once in his office, but at least that was after hours.

Preston and I walked hand in hand through the park, talking to people we knew. Everyone seemed to be having a great time.

On a whim, we decided to join the three-legged race. Preston, of course, had never participated in this rite of passage. We headed towards the starting line, joining several of his employees. I reached down, showing him how to tie our legs together and explaining the rules. When I stood back up I felt the telltale stabbing pain in my head that came before a psychic flash.

I gripped his forearm with one hand, my head with the other, as the vision assaulted my brain.

"What is it Meri? What do you see?" Preston asked. He no longer questioned my visions.

"I see...I see evil," I gasped.

The starter gun went off and racers pushed past us, heading towards the finish line. I was just about to suggest that we start running when we heard a voice behind us, cold enough to freeze fire.

"Preston Anderson Rutherford the third, what on Earth are you doing?"

We hopped around awkwardly, since our legs were stilled tied together, to greet an older couple who looked glaringly out of place at a picnic. The woman was wearing a pale blue suit with a white silk blouse and navy blue kitten heels. Her grey hair was pulled back in a bun so tight I wondered if it gave her a headache. Her thin lips pursed in disapproval as she looked us over. The resemblance was unmistakable. This had to be Preston's mother.

"Preston," she said to the man next to her. He was dressed in a dark blue suit with a vest and a tie, like he was going to work at the stock exchange. "Do you see your son? What is he wearing?"

"Son, who is this woman, and why are you tied to her?" his father asked, the word 'woman' clearly conveying something less flattering. "And wherever did you get those clothes? You look so...common."

Preston froze like a deer in the headlights, his gaze moving between his parents. I elbowed him in the side, bringing him back to the present.

"Mother. Father. This is my...friend Meri."

I suppressed the stab of hurt at being identified only as a friend. His parents looked at me like I was some bit of trash that got stuck to their shoe.

"Preston, we've talked about the type of women you see in private versus those you take out in public," his father chided.

There was no doubt which one I was.

"They sure grow them stout here in Colorado," his mother murmured just loud enough to make sure I heard.

If she thought I was going to wither under her insult, she hadn't been raised with sisters like mine. There was no insult she could hurl that would be more on the mark than anything I'd gotten from Cami or Pepper when we were fighting.

"I'm not stout, I'm an average sized woman," I told her firmly. "Nor am I someone to hide," I added, meeting his father's eyes. I thought I saw a flash of surprise. No doubt the Rutherfords were used to people kowtowing to them.

Preston was staring at a spot just past his mother's shoulder, looking like he wished he was anywhere else but here.

I reached down to untie the thick ribbon connecting our calves, feeling the loss of connection as soon as I stepped away. I had a bad feeling that our legs weren't the only thing breaking up.

I'd almost forgotten that Preston came from money and moved around in high society. We'd both gotten comfortable here in Greysden but seeing the shock and distaste on his parents' face reminded me that we were from completely different worlds. Maybe that's why I'd been hesitant to let him mark me – I'd always known that this wouldn't work out, no matter what his wolf wanted.

"I need to go check on the vendors," I told them. "If you'll excuse me."

"Meri, wait. Don't go."

I ignored Preston's plea and with my head held high, I walked across the park to see if I could hide in Gabriel's taco truck for a while.

Preston

I debated running after Meri versus dealing with my parents. If there was one thing I'd learned as the CEO of a large company, it was that you needed to deal with the most urgent crisis first.

"Why are you here?" I asked my parents. "I don't recall inviting you here."

Their eyes widened at my belligerent tone. I'd spent my entire life deferring to them, but my time in Colorado had opened my eyes. There was a whole different world out there, a world where people didn't judge you solely on your money and connections. And seeing Meri and her sisters with their parents had shown me what it was like to have parents who loved you for yourself, instead of as an accessory.

"I knew we shouldn't have let you move to this place," my mother replied dismissively. Why had I never noticed how grating and cold her tone was? It was so different than the warmth I got talking to Meri's mom.

"I'm forty-five years old, Mother. A grown man. I don't need you to 'let' me do anything. So, I'll ask you again, why are you here?"

"Is it so wrong for us to come visit our only son?" she asked, turning on the martyr voice. I resisted rolling my eyes, a habit I'd picked up from Meri, and waited her out.

"Fine. We heard through our sources that you seem to be losing your mind out here and forgetting who you are and where you come from. And seeing all this," she waved her hands around at the picnic, "I can see why they were concerned."

I made a mental note to ask Duncan to find out who was spying on me here so I could fire them.

"This is your idea of a company event, son?" my father piped up, his tone thick with disapproval. "It's so...common. And loud."

"It's a picnic, not a fundraising gala. People eat crappy food and play games at a picnic. It's an American tradition."

My mother sniffed in distaste. We were interrupted by Meri's mother who seemed to appear out of nowhere.

"Preston dear, this is a fabulous picnic."

She wrapped her arms around me and gave me a hug. Mrs. Rosewater didn't actually work at Rutherford Industries of course, but I'd invited all of Meri's family to join us as my guest. I was incredibly glad to see her here. I leaned into the warmth of her embrace. Never in my life had my own mother given me a hug like this.

"Thank you. I'm glad you could come."

"Who are these people?" Mrs. Rosewater asked curiously. My parents could not look more out of place here.

My mother's spine stiffened as she looked at Mrs. Rosewater with barely hidden distaste. Meri's mom was dressed in a short white dress covered with illustrations of herbs, their names printed beneath them. She had paired the dress with Birkenstocks and so many bracelets they ran halfway up her arm. Her hair was long and kind of wild.

"I'm Mrs. Preston Rutherford the second," my mother said icily. "Who are you?"

"Oh dear, are you so subjugated to your husband that you don't have your own name?"

My mother looked confused. When she didn't say more, Mrs. Rosewater turned her attention to my father.

"I take it you're Preston the second, then? I'm Sage Rosewater, Meri's mom."

"Who?"

"Meri, Preston's girlfriend."

My parents eyes snapped towards me completely in unison. "The woman you implied was fat earlier," I added helpfully.

Sage put her hands on her hips, immediately going mamma bear on them. "You called my baby fat?"

"I apologize," my mother said stiffly after a long pause. "We didn't realize she was someone...important."

"Everyone is important. I should hope you would know that at your age. Now, how long are you in town for?"

"A couple of days," Mother responded.

"Great, you'll come for dinner tomorrow night and meet the rest of the family. Preston will tell you how to get there, Goddess knows he's there enough. We'll see you tomorrow at six."

With that, she bustled away, leaving my parents looking slightly shellshocked. I resisted the urge to laugh at my parents being ordered around by a middle aged witch.

"Who was that woman?" my mother finally whispered, her tone a mix between horror and confusion.

"The mother of the woman I'm going to marry."

My mother gasped.

"Don't worry, you'll get used to them. Now if you'll excuse me, I need to find my girlfriend. I'll call you later, Mother."

Ignoring the look of outrage on my mother's face, I went in search of Meri. I found her playing an aggressive game of whack-a-mole against her sister Pepper.

That was one thing I'd learned about the Rosewater sisters over the past month: they were crazy competitive with each other. I still had nightmares about the game night I'd participated in with them. And possibly a scar.

"Another Rosewater crashing the Rutherford Industries picnic, I see," I teased Pepper.

"When you have something in the town square it becomes public," she retorted, never taking her eyes off the game. "Besides, you invited me, remember?"

"I know, I'm just teasing you."

The two sisters ignored me as they continued to play the game with the type of intense focus that was usually reserved for brain surgery or NASA space launches.

"Can we talk?" I whispered in Meri's ear.

She slammed a mallet over the head of a mole with enough force to shake the table. I felt my balls pull up closer to my body.

When she ignored me, I started to get irritated. I grabbed her by the waist and picked her up, pulling her smaller body against mine. She wiggled in my grasp.

"Hey!" she protested. "You just made me lose a game!"

"That's an unforgivable sin in the Rosewater family," Pepper added, "but thanks for helping me win."

"Put me down, Preston. Now!"

Meri kicked at my shins and when I ignored her, she headbutted me. The back of her skull connected with my nose, and I let her go as blood poured down my face.

"Ow! Damn it Meri, that hurt!" I roared. "I think you broke my nose!"

"Then don't manhandle me next time, asshole."

My girl was pissed. Rage was vibrating off of her in waves. Sick bastard that I was, it totally turned me on. My wolf was gloating about how strong our mate was, impressed with how she'd injured me.

"Are you two fighting?" Mrs. Rosewater appeared out of nowhere again. I wondered how she did that.

"No!" We both answered in unison.

Stepping closer, Mrs. Rosewater waved her hand in front of my face, murmuring something under her breath, and to my relief, my nose spontaneously healed.

"Wow, thank you."

"Just a little magic," she said smugly. "Now you two kiss and make up."

When we both stood there looking stubborn, she gave her daughter a chiding look.

"I just met Preston's parents, and he definitely needs us, Turmeric. Clearly that cold woman never gave him any love."

With that bit of wisdom, she wandered off, leaving us all staring after her.

"That was weird," I mumbled under my breath.

Pepper laughed behind us, and we turned in unison to give her a glare.

"I'll just be going now," she said, holding her hands up. "Bye."

"Are you still mad at me?" I asked Meri.

She rounded back on me, her face red with anger.

"Why would I be mad at you? After all, we're just friends." She sneered the word.

"I'm sorry, I thought it would make them leave you alone," I explained. "Those two can be brutal."

"Have you learned nothing hanging out with us Rosewaters?" she asked, pointing at my nose. "We can take care of ourselves."

I threaded my fingers through hers. "Lesson learned. After you left I made it clear that you were my girlfriend. I'm sorry I hurt your feelings. Can we go make up now?"

She sighed dramatically. "I guess. But I'm still annoyed with you."

"I'll make it up to you with orgasms."

"You'd better."

Meri

"This is a terrible idea."

Preston looked physically ill at the idea of having dinner with his parents. I couldn't blame him, they seemed like horrible people. Last night he'd opened up to me about his parents, and it gave me a unique insight into his background. Growing up with parents who were so focused on appearances and money had clearly shaped him into the man he was today.

I couldn't help but think that being turned into a wolf shifter had saved him. After all, it had brought him to Greysden where he'd learned to loosen up and be a regular person. It gave him the opportunity to experience love.

I stilled as I realized the truth. I loved Preston. I loved every fussy inch of him. I wondered if he'd ever feel the same way about me. I knew his wolf was on-board with our happily ever after, but Preston had kept his own feelings close to his vest. Now that I'd thought about it, he'd never expressed any emotion towards me, other than passion. I'd be lying if I said it didn't bother me.

I really hoped I wasn't alone in this. Yesterday when I thought Preston and I might break up, I'd been so upset I couldn't even eat Gabriel's tacos. That had never happened before.

"Nonsense," my mother responded to Preston. "This is a good idea. Your folks need to learn to loosen up and enjoy life, and we're just the family to do that."

My mother was nothing if not optimistic. I just hoped she was right.

A few minutes later the doorbell rang. Preston and I walked hand in hand to answer the door. His parents stood stiffly on the porch, dressed like they were going to a board meeting instead of a casual dinner.

"Mother, Father," he greeted them. "I'd like to introduce you to my *girlfriend* Meri."

His mother's eye twitched but to her credit she reached her hand out. "Pleased to meet you."

His father extended his hand next, and the minute he touched me I gasped, overwhelmed with a vision. I winced with the jolt of pain that shot through my head.

"Jo-Jo didn't go to a farm," I told him as the vision became clear. "Your mother took him to the pound."

All the color drained out of Mr. Rutherford's face. "How do you know about Jo-Jo?"

"Who's Jo-Jo?" both Preston and Mrs. Rutherford asked at the same time.

"She was a stray dog I found when I was a young boy," he explained. "She was so cute and affectionate, but my mother didn't want to have a dog. I came home from school one day and she was gone. Mother said she'd taken her to a farm in the country. She said Jo-Jo would be happier there than living in the city."

Having met Preston's family, I can't say I was shocked that his mother would steal his dog and lie about it. Poor kid, no wonder he grew up to be like he was. For a second I thought the older man might start crying, but then he pulled himself together. His shocked gaze locked on mine.

"How did you know?"

"She's psychic," Preston said, as if it were the most natural thing in the world. "Shall we meet the rest of the family?"

We took the Rutherfords into the parlor, introducing them to my father, my two sisters, and Cami's mate Stephen. Of course they'd already met my mother.

Mom gave the Rutherfords each a hug – much to their obvious discomfort—and we all sat down. Preston sat in one of the armchairs, pulling me on his lap and ignoring the disapproving looks he got from his parents. I snuggled against him, reveling in his easy affection. Maybe he felt more for me than he let on?

After getting everyone's drink orders, Dad handed Mrs. Rutherford a glass of white wine. Suddenly he stilled, his face contorting with a vision.

"Your maid didn't steal your ring, it fell behind your dresser, right against the baseboard," he told her, his voice turning hard. "You fired that poor girl for nothing."

Mrs. Rutherford flinched. "Is the whole family psychic?" she asked.

"No, of course not," Dad answered. "Meri and I are the only psychics. Cami is a witch like Sage, but Pepper didn't inherit any of our gifts unfortunately. And Stephen here is a wolf, like your son is now."

Mrs. Rutherford knocked back her glass of wine like it was a shot of whiskey.

"Is this one of those internet shows?" Mrs. Rutherford asked. "Is some young man with a camera going to jump out and yell at us?"

"You're funny," Mom laughed, as if she'd been joking.

"Wait, what did he mean about wolves?" Mr. Rutherford asked, his eyes swinging towards Preston.

"Mother. Father. I know this is going to come as a shock, but there's a whole supernatural world that exists, right alongside the human world."

His mother gasped.

"One night when I was in New York, I was jumped by a gang of rogue wolves. One of them bit me and turned me into a shape shifter, which means I'm sharing my body with a wolf now. That's why I really moved to Greysden, to learn how to live as a shifter."

"Greysden is a shifter sanctuary town," I added.

"Are you having some kind of a breakdown?" Mrs. Rutherford asked Preston shrilly. "Is there something in the water in this town that makes everyone insane?"

"You'd better show them your wolf, it'll be easier," Mom suggested. "Let's go into the yard."

Leaving the siblings behind, both sets of parents followed me and Preston to the back yard. Preston pulled off his clothes, ignoring his mother's outraged cries, and with a long exhale, shifted into his wolf form. He'd been working with both Stephen and his friend Duncan, and his shifting skills had improved a lot the last few weeks. I suspected it helped that he was no longer fighting against it.

Mrs. Rutherford sat down hard on the back stairs, her legs collapsing in shock. Preston's wolf padded over to her, nudging her with his head. She shrieked when they made contact. Her husband put his hand on her shoulder, watching Preston carefully.

"It is you, isn't it, son?"

Preston's wolf nodded its head.

"Well, isn't that the damnedest thing?" He sounded bemused, and not as surprised as I would think he would be. He'd obviously heard whispers about shifters somewhere before. Or maybe he knew more than he was letting on.

"Preston! Change back into a man at once!" his mother ordered. "We're taking you back to New York to get help. There must be a doctor who can help you be normal again."

The air shimmered, and the sound of bones and muscles reshaping filled the air as Preston changed back into his human form. He pulled on his shorts and t-shirt before turning to his parents.

"I don't want help, Mother, and I'm not going back to New York. I like my new life here."

"You're clearly not mentally stable, son, if you want to live like this," his father stated. "This...whatever happened to you, must have impacted your mind. You've not been acting like yourself, living here among these crazies, and forgetting your roots."

He waved his hand at Preston's shorts and tee shirt.

"If the press saw you, dressed like that, turning into a wolf, my God, the family would be ruined. You'll either come back with us and allow us to get you some help, or we'll go to the board and have you removed from the CEO position at Rutherford Industries."

Preston's face hardened, instantly going from the relaxed guy he'd been all month back to the cold CEO.

"I've got bad news for you Father. I've been purchasing additional shares of the company for years. I'm the majority shareholder of Rutherford Industries now, which means I have the deciding vote on any board decisions. You can't touch me or the company."

He walked over and put his arm around my shoulder. "But even if you could push me out of the company, I'd still stay here with Meri. There's no way I'd leave the woman I love."

I gasped. "You love me?"

"Of course I love you. You're my mate."

Disappointment stabbed me like a knife. "Oh, you mean your wolf loves me."

He turned me around to face him, standing quietly until I looked up to meet his tender gaze.

"My wolf loves you and so does my human side. You're everything to me, Meri. I'd love you even if my wolf went away tomorrow. You're my soulmate."

I heard my mother sigh happily behind me.

"Really?" I asked hopefully.

I could see the truth in his eyes. "Really."

"In that case, how about you take me upstairs and give me your mark?"

His eyes widened in understanding. "You're ready to officially be my mate?"

"Try and stop me."

He picked me up with a whoop and threw me over his shoulder.

"Mother, Father, I'll see you later. Mrs. Rosewater, I think we'll have to take a pass on dinner."

My mother laughed. "Call me Sage dear. And welcome to the family."

Epilogue - Preston

One year later...

"This is the best company picnic you've ever planned for us."

"It's only the second one," Meri replied. "There's not a lot to compare it to."

I leaned down and pressed a kiss on the top of her head. "I don't care, it's still fabulous. I'm so proud of you."

Meri had expanded the event this year, adding more games, more activities, and more food offerings. We'd been inundated with local businesses wanting to participate in the event. We'd also hired a band and set up a large area for people to dance.

The crowd was a mix of local Greysden residents and people who worked for my company.

Meri paused, gripping her head, as a vision hit her.

"What is it?" I asked.

"I don't know. I just had a flash of a man with horns and red eyes. It looked like he was at a Halloween party somewhere, but the horns were real. It doesn't make sense."

Meri's visions had improved in both clarity and accuracy over the last year, although she still had what she called her "useless psychic flashes". Her mother attributed her more reliable skills to being in a stable relationship with her soul mate. My wolf had preened when he heard that, thrilled that our love had helped our mate.

My own shifter skills were better too. Once we'd sealed the deal and officially mated with Meri, my wolf had calmed down considerably. We mostly were in sync now, which was a relief after our tumultuous beginnings.

"Do you need to rest?" I asked my wife solicitously.

My wife. It made me as happy to say that as it made my wolf to say, *my mate.* Whatever you called her, Meri was ours. And we were hers.

After I'd marked her last year, activating the mate bond, I'd officially moved into Meri's suite at the Rosewater Manor. I felt much more comfortable there than my old apartment on the top floor of my office building. And after growing up in the cold and formal home I'd shared with my parents, I loved the controlled chaos and exuberant love of the Rosewater home.

Six months after we mated we'd gotten married, making our relationship as official in the human world as it already was in the shifter world. We'd chosen to get married in a small intimate ceremony in the backyard of Rosewater estate. Meri's sisters had been her co-maids of honor, and Duncan had been my best man.

My parents had come down from New York and to my surprise, seemed to have fun. Sage had taken them under her wing, and with her charm and liberal servings of alcohol, they'd "gotten the stick out of their asses", as Pepper had proclaimed. At least until they'd left.

"Being pregnant doesn't make me an invalid, you know," Meri responded.

Last month Meri had shocked the hell out of me by announcing that she was pregnant. We hadn't been actively trying, but she'd gotten her IUD out the month before, and we hadn't been taking any other precautions either. She'd gotten pregnant way faster than we'd expected, but needless to say, we were thrilled at the idea of being parents.

If Cami and Stephen's experience with their twins was any indication, it was going to be a wild ride. Their kids appeared to have both shifter and magic skills, and even though they weren't even a year old, they were already a handful. I suspected a vasectomy was in Stephen's future.

All the Rosewater sisters had settled down – even Pepper had finally found her true love, although it had been a hell of a wild ride.

Best of all, Meri's event planning business had picked up enough for her to give up both her pet sitting gigs and her shifts at Bearly Beans.

She still worked one day a week at Rosewater's Magical Emporium, but that was more for Cami than for the money. Not that Meri needed to work, not when she was married to a billionaire, but she'd told me in no uncertain terms that she was going to retain her independence. I respected the hell out of her for that.

"Can I have this dance?"

Meri gave me a soft smile. "I was hoping you would ask."

I led her onto the floor and pulled her into my arms. As always, everything inside me calmed as she melted against me, her curves fitting perfectly against my body. Deep inside me, my wolf chuffed happily.

I sent a smile to Duncan, who was dancing with his own mate on the other side of the floor. I wasn't the only wolf who'd found his mate here in Greysden.

Moving to this town was the best decision I'd ever made. And as I danced with my love, dreaming about our child on the way, I knew that the best was yet to come.

*** Keep reading for Pepper's Story "Kitchen Magic" ***

Kitchen Magic

The Magical Midlife Series
By
Rose Bak

Copyright

About This Book

Just when she'd given up on finding her fated mate, he turns up in her kitchen.

Pepper Rosewater is known around town as the "mate magnet". Everyone in the magical town of Greysden seems to find their true love when they're with Pepper. Shifters, demons, witches...she helps them all, whether she means to or not.

Now she's decided to focus on her newly restored witchcraft and do something she's always longed to do – learn how to cook.

Charles is a magical mutt. He's part demon, part wolf, part vampire, and one hundred percent grumpy about it. Ever since he turned forty his mother had been trying to marry him off in increasingly annoying ways, so when his cousin tells him about a head chef job at a new restaurant, the confirmed bachelor jumps at the chance to relocate.

But everything is not as it seems in his new town...His rental burned down, forcing him to accept the offer of a room at Rosewater Manor. The four-star restaurant he expected is really more like a diner, with a training kitchen in the back. And one of his new culinary students hates him on sight, which is a big problem considering that Pepper isn't just his new roommate—she's also his mate.

"Kitchen Magic" is a steamy midlife paranormal romantic comedy featuring a wise-cracking woman finding her magic, a cranky chef who's learning you can't fight fate, and a small town full of matchmakers who are determined to help them find their happily ever after.

About the "Magical Midlife" series: Just outside the shifter town of Greysden sits Rosewater Manor, a place shrouded in magic. The Rosewater women and their friends all have special gifts, although sometimes they're a bit glitchy. At least until they find true love...

Dedication

For everyone who's been tempted to give up on finding true love. Maybe you'll find your own monster...

Prologue—Pepper

Two years ago...

We were all gathered around the fire, trying to reverse the disastrous love spell my sister Cami had done. It had been intended to attract a mate for me to love, but somehow my dear old sister had managed to call a mate for herself instead. A smoking hot wolf shifter to boot. I would have totally gone for him if the dumb dog wasn't hopelessly in love with my sister. Stephen believed that fate had brought them together, but Cami wanted to be sure it wasn't just the love potion, so she was having our mother reverse her faulty spell.

My sisters and I gathered around the fire with my mother and Stephen, sitting within the circle lines my mother drew in the dirt. I grabbed Cami's hand, then reached for my little sister Meri with my other hand. The minute our hands touched, Meri gasped loudly, going stiff as a board, a sure sign she was having one of her psychic visions. The problem with her visions is you never knew what you were going to get. She could be seeing my death or locating my lost earring.

"What is it?" I asked. "What do you see?"

Meri rubbed her forehead, her eyes going glassy as a vision flashed in her mind. "A monster!"

We all stared at her as she mumbled incoherently for a few seconds. Her gaze cleared and she swung her head around to stare at me in shock.

"Pepper! Your true love is a monster!"

"What are you talking about?"

A wave of panic hit me. I grabbed her hand again and squeezed—hard.

"Are you saying I'm going to fall in love with a terrible person? What the hell? Why do I keep getting bad news in this damn forest?"

"I don't know." Meri shook her head, as if clearing it. "I saw you in my vision, we were all in the library, and you were telling us you were in love, but he was a monster. Then I saw of flash of...something, I don't know what it was. Some weird creature. Then it was gone."

I sighed deeply as our mother brought our attention back to reversing Cami's love spell. My mate was going to be a monster? Yeah, that seemed about on par for my life.

Pepper

"Hey Pepper, how are your magic lessons going?"

I smiled at my old school mate Janice who was back in town for her parents' anniversary. We met for lunch at Murphy's Bar to grab a drink and catch up. Behind the bar, wolf shifter Marie was bickering with her bear shifter mate, Ben. Those two bickered non-stop – when they weren't having sex in the back room. They totally had that enemies to lovers vibe going for them.

"My lessons are going okay I guess," I told my friend, resting my chin on my hand. "When I heard that my crazy aunt had accidentally suppressed my magic, I guess I thought it would just surge back and I'd be some kick-ass witch. Instead, I'm taking beginner witch lessons with middle schoolers."

I wasn't kidding either. This morning my mother taught me and five kids ages nine to twelve how to change the color of our shoes. I was the only one who couldn't quite get it, thus the reason why I was currently wearing a pair of keds that looked like a paint store had thrown up on them.

"Cami sucked at magic for a long time," Janice reminded me.

It was true. My sister's magic had gotten better once she'd mated with Stephen, but it still wasn't as good as our mother's. Sage Rosewater was one of the most powerful witches in the region. It was a big legacy to live up to.

"Maybe you're trying too hard," Janice suggested. "Sometimes you just have to relax and let the magic come in its own time."

Janice was a wolf shifter thanks to her father, but her mother was a witch in the same coven as my mom, so she knew what she was talking about.

"I'm going to be forty in a couple of years," I reminded her. "There's not a lot of time left to wait."

"Forty is the new twenty," Janice said. "Besides, you're only thirty-seven."

I took a drink of my beer and sighed. "Maybe I should give up on learning more magic and focus on another hobby."

"Like what?"

I rolled my eyes up towards the ceiling as I thought about her question.

"I've always wanted to take cooking classes. They're opening a culinary school here in Greysden and offering classes for the general public. Maybe I'll take some classes to keep my mind occupied."

"Ooh, maybe you'll find out that you're a kitchen witch," Janice said excitedly. "That would be cool. You'll be able to create gourmet meals with the wag of a finger."

"My cooking is worse than my magic. I can scarcely boil water," I said drily. "I'm guessing that won't be my calling."

Suddenly my friend stiffened in her seat, her nostrils flaring. A second later I heard a low growl.

"Mine!"

I looked over Janice's shoulder to see a strange man stalking towards us, his eyes fixed on my friend. Like she was in a trance or something, Janice got up and turned to meet the man.

He stopped about six inches away from her, a look of wonder on his face. "Mate! I've finally found you."

Janice growled in response. "Mine!"

I slouched down in my seat and drained the rest of my beer. Once again, I was with someone when they found their fated mate. I was like a human metal detector, except instead of locating lost rings, I found people's fated mate. It had happened so often that people in town were now calling me 'the mate finder'.

My friend left the table without a word, not even taking her purse. Janice grabbed the stranger's hand and they took off at a fast jog, no doubt to find a quiet place to mate and mark each other.

"I can't believe this is happening to me again," I said miserably as I watched them go. "Always the mate finder, never the mated."

I gestured for Marie to bring me another beer. She hustled over, giving me a curious smile.

"What happened to Janice?" she asked. "She left in a hurry."

"She found her mate."

Marie cocked her head. "It happened again, huh? Don't worry Pepper, sooner or later your mate will come for you."

I gave her what I hoped was a reassuring smile.

"It's fine. I think I'm just going to focus on myself for a while. I mean, Meri had a vision a few years ago that my mate was a monster anyway, so who wants that?"

"Yeah, but Meri's visions have always been a little wonky," she reminded me. "Maybe monster meant something else."

"Like what?"

"I don't know, I'm just saying that, personally, I wouldn't put a lot of stock in an old vision from an unreliable psychic gift. She hasn't seen anything about your mate recently, right?"

"Right."

Of course, my sister was too busy banging her mate Preston. Even after nearly two years together, those two couldn't seem to get enough of each other. I'd walked in on them in delicate situations so many times I was considering getting therapy.

Marie reached forward and squeezed my shoulder. "You're going to be all right Pepper, even if you don't find someone. You're a strong woman. You don't need a mate to make you complete."

We both turned as Ben growled at some guy who was checking out Marie's ass. The bear was notoriously possessive of his mate – much to her irritation.

"See?" Marie said. "Mates are more trouble than they're worth sometimes."

Charles

I scented the female the minute I opened the door to my apartment. A wolf from the smell of her. Following my nose, I found the female in my bedroom, laying on my bed wearing only a very skimpy teddy and a predatory smile.

"Hi, big guy."

I rolled my eyes. "Get out."

"But, your mother sent me to—."

"I don't care what my mother told you," I interrupted, "or why she thought it was okay to let you into my condo. Leave now, and when you report back to my mother, be sure to tell her I'm changing the locks."

The woman pouted. The truth was, she was attractive. Very attractive, despite what appeared to be surgically enhanced tits. But there were two problems. First, I didn't want a woman who would put on sexy lingerie and hang out in a strange man's bedroom hoping to trap him. Second, I didn't want a mate. Ever.

That was something my mother just couldn't understand. She'd been happily mated to my father for over forty years, and she wanted me to have the same domestic bliss that they did.

Sure, I was part of the supernatural world and all supes were obsessed with the fated mate thing. But I was a mutt. The son of a female demon whose fated mate was the son of a wolf shifter and a vampire, I didn't fit in anywhere in the world. Not completely. And when I shifted into my animal, well, let's just say it wasn't pretty. I'd seen pictures, and even I had been repulsed by the sight of the hybrid being that lived inside me. I totally understood why other shifters got freaked out by it.

My mother, romantic that she was, figured that fate and I both needed a nudge. Growing up she'd always told me that when I found my fated mate, he or she would think my animal was perfect just like he was, like some kind of Beauty and the Beast scenario.

Ever since I turned forty earlier this year she'd shoved all manner of females in front of me in increasingly sneaky ways, hoping that if I didn't find my fated mate, maybe I'd still find a compatible female to make my life with. My mother was dying for grandchildren, and I was her only hope.

Every time I went to my parents' house, some supe's daughter just 'happened' to be there. When we went out to dinner, there was always a strange female joining us. My mother had even brought females to meet me at the restaurant where I was a chef several times but this, parking a willing female in my bed, well, it was a step too far.

The woman stalked towards me, pointing her ample cleavage in my direction.

"I know we're not mates, but maybe we can have some fun anyway?" she said hopefully, her talon like nails dragging down the fabric of my shirt.

"Out. Now."

I didn't have it in me to be polite tonight. It had been a long day and my mother's matchmaking attempts were on my last nerve. Why couldn't she leave me in peace?

As I escorted the wolf out of my apartment and locked the door behind her, I thought back to an email my cousin Duncan sent me yesterday. He lived in a town in Colorado called Greysden where just about everyone was a supe. Apparently, wolves, fae, vampires, witches, demons, and even an alien lived in harmony in the little town in the mountains, all of them able to be completely open about their dual natures.

After a lifetime hiding my true nature in the city, it sounded like heaven.

Duncan forwarded me a job posting for the director of an exciting new venture in Greysden. Wolf Kitchens was a restaurant that would be an incubator for its culinary training program. Student chefs would work alongside the professionals to get real world experience in the culinary arts. The director would serve as both as the restaurant's general manager and lead culinary instructor, managing both staff and faculty as well as having high level oversight of the menu.

It was an exciting opportunity, and one that paid well. Maybe I should pursue it? Besides the fact that my mother was driving me crazy, I'd been unhappy at work lately. The restaurant had sold to a new owner and while they'd kept me and the rest of the staff on during the transition, it was becoming increasingly clear that my vision and the new owner's did not mesh.

It didn't hurt to explore my options. Maybe something new and exciting waited for me in Greysden...

***

Two months later....

"Welcome to Greysden, man!"

My cousin Duncan pulled me into a big hug. Second cousins on my mother's side, we used to be pretty tight back when he lived in New York, but a few years ago he'd moved back to his hometown of Greysden. His human boss, billionaire CEO Preston Rutherford the third, had been bitten by rogue shifters and turned into a wolf. My cousin was Rutherford's security chief and seeing his boss struggle with his new shifter side, he'd suggested that they all relocate to Greysden where it was safe for Rutherford to explore his furry side.

Duncan put his arm around a pretty wolf shifter. "Charles, this is my mate, Elizabeth. Elizabeth, my cousin Charles."

Duncan had met his mate here in Greysden after she'd run away from a forced wedding in some archaic wolf pack she used to be a part of back in Montana. It had been love at first sight for him, but Elizabeth had taken a little bit longer to come around. It was clear my cousin was head over heels for her though. He was looking at her like she hung the damned moon.

"Welcome to Greysden, Charles," Elizabeth said warmly. "I've heard a lot about you and hope you'll be as happy here as we are."

"Maybe you'll finally meet your mate," Duncan added. "There are a lot of unmated females in Greysden."

I growled. "Now don't you start that shit with me too."

My cousin laughed. "Sorry, your mama already called and gave me an earful about how thanks to me you're leaving her and now you'll never find your fated mate."

I rolled my eyes. "Yeah, I've been hearing that ever since I told her I was moving."

"She perked up when I told her that I knew a lot of females looking for mates," Duncan told me.

I took a deep breath and smiled. "Wow, the air is so fresh and clean here, I'm already feeling better about my life."

"Yeah, I don't miss the polluted air in New York, that's for sure," Duncan agreed. "Now let's get you to your rental house so you can settle in. I have a feeling that you're going to love it here. There's no better place to live than Greysden."

Pepper

"That's it Pepper, try to hold it there just a little bit longer."

My mother watched as I levitated a boulder that had fallen near the river running along the edge of our property. When I started getting my magic powers back a year ago last Halloween, I'd only been able to levitate a pencil. Lifting a giant boulder was progress. Slow progress, but progress. Letting the magic flow through me, I moved the boulder from one place to another.

"What are you guys doing?"

The boulder crashed to the ground as my sister's cheerful voice came from behind us.

"Damn it, Meri! You ruined my concentration!"

"Sorry, Sis. Dad sent me out to tell you two that dinner is ready. Preston and I got here a little while ago, and Cami and Stephen are here with the twins."

I perked up. I loved those little terrors. My niece and nephew were half witch, half wolf shifter, and at only twelve months old, they were already quite a handful. I couldn't wait to see what trouble they got into when they were older.

My mother and I turned to follow Meri, and my sister affectionately slung her arm over my shoulder. Despite our very different personalities, my two sisters and I had always been close. With a mother who was a powerful witch and a father who was a world-famous psychic, the Rosewater family was a bit strange, even by Greysden standards. We grew up in my mother's family's ancestral home, Rosewater Manor, and while Meri and Cami had moved out with their mates, I still lived at home.

It wasn't as weird as it seemed. The Manor was huge, and I had my own wing. Between that and my parents' frequent travels, I honestly didn't see a whole lot of them. Most of the time, I had the place to myself, which was good because I worked at home doing freelance graphic design, and that required a lot of concentration.

It would require less concentration if you could use magic to help, the little voice in the back of my brain snarked. I ignored it. I was doing my best, but maybe it was just too late for me to develop any level of magical competency. At least I had some limited magic powers now after so many years of believing I was the only person in my family without any special talents. It was definitely getting easier to harness my powers.

When Meri and my mom and I got back to the house, everyone was already gathered around the large wooden table in the dining room waiting for us. When my parents were in town, my mother and father insisted that we have a family dinner at least once a week.

Rosewater Manor had been in my mother's family for nearly two hundred years. Rosewaters lived on this land long before the gray wolves founded the shifter town of Greysden up the road. It was a beautiful old house with hardwood floors, crown molding, and generations of Rosewater history in every room. My favorite was the parlor, an old-fashioned room filled with antique furniture, magical tools and spell books, and generations of family photographs.

"Hey everyone," I greeted the assembled crew. I dropped a kiss on the heads of my niece and nephew, then slid into the remaining chair.

My dad had prepared a giant pot roast along with roasted root vegetables, a salad, rice, and bread. The two shifters in the family, Preston and Stephen, practically attacked the food. With their shifter metabolisms, they were always ravenous. And not only for food, I thought, as I noticed Preston's non-eating hand disappear under the table in the vicinity of my sister's upper thigh.

"Did you hear that the town council hired a director for Wolf Kitchens?" Cami asked. "Duncan came into the shop today to look for a gift for Elizabeth, and he told me his cousin from New York took the job. He's some big time French chef who was looking for a change."

'The shop' was Rosewater Emporium, my family's store in downtown Greysden. It sold books, mystical items, and gifts. Like our house, it predated the town.

"Duncan's cousin is French?" Dad asked.

"No, I mean he specializes in French cuisine," Cami responded. "Although that might be a bit fancy for us here in Greysden."

Like most places in Colorado, Greysden liked good, simple food, preferably locally sourced. You had to drive forty-five minutes down the mountain to get anything resembling fast food.

"Oh good, I'm glad they finally hired someone," I said. "I'm signed up to take their intro to cooking lessons as soon as they open. Janice's new mate Donald was hired as head chef, but they wanted to wait for the director to start so he could create the curriculum for the classes."

"You're taking cooking lessons?" my mother asked. She seemed surprised, no doubt due to my complete disinterest in cooking over the years.

"I want to. It would be nice to be able to make something besides cereal and macaroni and cheese when you guys are out of town. Besides, I thought it would be good to take up a hobby to keep my mind off my lack of magic skills."

Mom gave me a sympathetic look. "Your skills are coming along Pepper, you just need to be patient. If only we knew what my sister had done earlier, when it was easier for you to learn..."

My Aunt Pat grew up here at Rosewater Manor along with my mother, but she'd always been ashamed of her family. When she went away to college, she married a strict Christian who thought magic was a sin, and Aunt Pat stopped using her powers. When her infant daughter Jane showed signs of being a witch, Aunt Pat did a suppression spell to bind her magic. Unfortunately, I was in the same room at the time, and my magic was suppressed too. For years my cousin and I thought we were 'normals', as we called the non-magical non-supernatural humans.

Right around Jane's fortieth birthday, she suddenly started getting her magic back, which was how the truth came out about Aunt Pat's shenanigans. My cousin lived in Greysden now. She moved here after she mated with Duncan's half-brother Gabriel, who declared that Jane was his mate when she went to a Halloween party with me. Another Pepper Rosewater mate connection.

With my mother's help, my cousin had become a kickass witch. Unlike me.

"There's no sense rehashing what happened with Aunt Pat," I told my mother. "It is what it is. I'll never be as good as you or Jane. I'm not even as good as Glitchy Spell Cami here—."

"Hey!" my sister protested. Cami's skills had improved dramatically since she and Stephen had mated, but she was still just as likely to turn you into a frog as create a puff of smoke.

"As I was saying, I may never be a badass witch, or find a mate of my own, but that doesn't mean I can't have a full life. I'll keep working on my magic and learn how to cook and hell, maybe I'll get a cat or something. In the meantime, I'm just going to have to be happy helping everyone else find their mate."

"Oh yeah, I heard that new cashier at the drug store found her mate while she was ringing up your order the other day," Meri said sympathetically. "It was nice of the manager to give you free dental floss after that happened."

Charles

"This is Wolf Kitchens?" I said dubiously.

The restaurant and culinary training program were housed inside a large building at the very edge of Main Street in downtown Greysden. Two restaurants used to be housed side by side here, but then the space had sat empty for many years until the town council had the idea of creating a culinary training kitchen and what they deemed to be a "nice" restaurant.

The building looked more like a diner than a four-star restaurant. Vinyl covered booths ringed the space, with a couple of dozen basic tables and chairs arranged in the center. There was a bar on one side and what looked like a lunch counter on the other. A soda machine sat in the corner, a stack of cups lined up neatly next to it. Through the open window I could see someone working in the kitchen lifting a basket of fries out of hot oil.

I was glad to see that the kitchen was clean, but glancing at the proposed menu, I could see that the food was decidedly uninspired. This would not do. No restaurant I was in charge of was going to serve meatloaf and hamburgers, let alone French fries.

I took a few minutes to meet the skeleton staff that had been hired before I got here: a head chef, two sous chefs, and a bus boy who also was the dishwasher. When we were ready to open, we'd have to hire a couple of waitresses too.

I pulled out my phone and started making a list of everything I was going to need to do to get this place in tip top condition. Tablecloths. Upholstered booths to replace the vinyl. Better lighting. Removing that damned lunch counter. Oh, and a complete overhaul of the menu.

Donald, the head chef, looked over my shoulder as I tapped out a list.

"Oh good, I hate the menu too," he said, giving me hope. "So far we've just been adding whatever random shit people ask for and selling carryout lunch for the locals."

He rolled his eyes. "The people of Greysden don't have the most refined palates, I need to warn you about that ahead of time."

"Good to know." I looked at him, noting that he was a wolf shifter. He was a big, burly guy with red hair and a matching beard. "Are you originally from Greysden?" I asked.

"No, I grew up in Denver and have been working in restaurants in the city since I graduated culinary school. I came here to visit a friend two months ago and found my mate while I was here, so I decided to relocate."

He pointed to the mark at the juncture of his neck. "She's a wolf too. Great gal."

"Congratulations."

The happy expression on his face when Donald talked about his mate made my heart pinch. Before we could say anything else, Mabel, one of the geriatric board members who'd hired me, rushed in with a big smile.

"Charles! So glad you made it. Welcome to Greysden." She shook my hand, and I pegged her as a wolf. "Your class begins in five minutes."

"Class? What class?"

"Basic Cooking Skills."

I frowned. "We already have culinary students?" I asked incredulously. "Today's my first day. I haven't even started working on curriculum."

"Oh no, this is our community class for adults who want to learn how to cook. It's a ninety-minute class and you have ten students over in the culinary kitchen waiting for you."

When I just stared at her she clapped her hands. "Chop chop. You need to teach those people how to chop chop."

Laughing at her own joke, she hustled away. I turned to look at Donald, who shrugged.

"I told her to wait until you'd gotten settled in, but she ignored me and told everyone to come in for their first lesson. Then again, it's a bunch of people who don't know how to boil water or roast a chicken. How hard can it be?"

Shaking my head, I followed Donald to the culinary kitchen that had been built on the other side of the building. The closer I got, the weirder I felt. My animal side, which was usually quiet inside me as long as I let it out to run every once in a while, suddenly woke up and bashed around inside me excitedly.

"What's wrong?" I asked.

"She's here!" my animal said excitedly. It felt like he was turning around in circles in my chest.

"Who?"

There was no answer, just a lot of excited yipping and howling. My animal had some characteristics from both my demon side and my wolf side, as well as some of the personality traits of my vampire side. It was confusing, to say the least. Or, as my mother always told me, I had a very unique animal.

Last night I'd gone out for a drink with Duncan and met his half-brother Gabriel, another cousin who I'd only become aware of about a year ago. He'd come to Greysden after his mother died to meet his long-lost father and found a friend in his newly discovered half-brother Duncan. Gabe was a demon wolf hybrid and we'd clicked immediately. The two of us clicked immediately, and it was interesting to talk to him about the ways he managed and balanced his disparate animal sides. I'd never met another hybrid before, usually if two different species mated, their child turned into one or the other.

Pushing open the door to the training kitchen I stiffened as I was assaulted with the sweetest smell. It was like violets, mixed with something I couldn't define. I looked around, absently taking in the stainless steel counters and high-end appliances in the room. The culinary kitchen was more modern and equipped than the restaurant for some reason. I couldn't wait to train new chefs here.

My attention fixed on a beautiful dark-haired woman standing behind a table in the back of the room. With my animal pushing to get out, I made a beeline for her, inhaling subtly. What was my animal so excited about?

The woman wasn't a shifter. I could sense a little magic around her, but not very strong. Maybe she was a fae or some other kind of supe. She was a little thing, maybe five four, with generous curves that were visible even beneath the apron she'd pulled over her clothes. Glancing at her face, I estimated that she was in her mid-thirties, a few years younger than me. She had long, thick dark brown hair, pale white skin, a slightly upturned nose, and a mouth I couldn't wait to kiss.

As if she heard my thoughts, her piercing gray blue eyes flew to mine. She looked a little shocked, like maybe she was feeling the same strange pull as me. What was happening? I felt excited and sick and freaked out all at the same time. A low growl rumbled in my chest as I continued to stare at her.

"Mine!" my animal screeched inside me. *"Mine! This woman is our mate! Claim her! Claim her now!"*

I shook my head, trying to calm the animal down.

"No," I said firmly. "Not her. Not now."

Pepper

I had no idea what was wrong with this guy. He barreled into the classroom like a man on a mission, coming right up to hover over me. He looked me over from head to toe, making me shiver, and then he sneered at me like he'd smelled something bad. When he growled, "no, not her," everyone in the room turned to stare at me. My face flamed with embarrassment.

"Hey, have you ever heard of personal space?" I asked. "Step back."

He stepped back, but said, "You can't be here."

"I paid for this class the same as everyone else," I told him. "I have every right to be here. Now are you going to teach us how to cook or do we need to all get our money back?"

He stared at me for another weighted moment before turning around to head to the front of the class. I saw Donald, my friend Janice's new mate, standing in the corner of the room. He gave me a little wave, then turned a thoughtful gaze back towards the surly man.

When the strange man who'd tried to intimidate me just stood there looking like he'd seen a ghost, Donald clapped his hands to get our attention.

"Hello everyone, most of you know me, but for those who don't, I'm Donald, the head chef here. I'd like to introduce you to the new Director of Wolf Kitchens, Charles Fields. Chef Fields is classically trained in French cuisine, and most recently was the head chef at La Petite Pigeon in New York City. Please welcome him to Greysden."

The other students gave Charles a polite round of applause, which seemed to rouse him out of his stupor. He strode to the front of the room, and I subtly checked him out. He might be rude, but he was hot. Movie star hot.

He was tall, a few inches over six feet, although that wasn't super tall by Greysden standards where almost every other guy was a shifter of some sort. They grew them big here.

157

Charles had thick, inky black hair parted on the side in some kind of a swoop, the bottom a couple of inches past his ears. He looked like he used hair gel, which I totally hated on a guy. His eyes were brown and intense under thick dark eyebrows, and the thick layer of scruff on his jaw gave him a dangerous air. Or maybe that was the scowl that darkened up his handsome face.

You could tell just looking at this guy that he was intense. I wondered how all that intensity would play out in the bedroom before I resolutely got my mind out of the gutter. I wasn't sure what I'd done to that guy, but it was painfully obvious that he didn't like me very much. That was fine, I didn't like him either.

"Okay everyone, sorry for the delay. The first part of our lesson will be on kitchen safety. Who here has had any knife skills training?"

When no one raised their hands, Charles pulled out some knives and started to demonstrate. As we went through the knife skills unit and moved onto the uses of other kitchen tools, I couldn't help but notice that Charles was completely ignoring me. He studiously avoided looking my way, and I was the only person he didn't come over to assist with the knives, even though I was totally struggling.

The longer class went on, the angrier I became. By the time was we were finished, I was full-on mad. I waited for the other students to leave, then stormed up to the front of the room. I dumped a pile of mutilated vegetables on the table with a thud.

"What's your problem with me?" I asked.

He stared at the stainless steel table in front of him.

"I don't have a problem with you," he mumbled.

"I think you do," I said stubbornly. "You think I didn't notice the way you ignored me the entire class? You're supposed to be teaching me, the same as everyone else. We've never met before today, so I know there's no way I pissed you off. Yet you can't even look me in the eye right now."

His head snapped up, mouth set in a firm, angry line. Almost as if it was against his will, his eyes met mine. Something passed between us, and I felt a jolt run through my body, as if he'd sent out an electrical shock using only his eyes. Involuntarily, I took a step back, breaking eye contact. My breath was coming in short pants, but I couldn't for the life of me say why.

"What...what was that?" I asked. "Are you a warlock or something? Did you just put a spell on me?"

He laughed, but there was no humor there. "No, a warlock is pretty much the only kind of supe I don't have inside me."

"Huh?"

I could practically see him restraining himself from rolling his eyes. Charles was a snob, that much was clear, from his expensive clothes to his styled hair to the look of arrogant disdain he'd given when he walked into the classroom at Wolf Kitchens.

"I think it might be better if I refund your class fees," he said, his tone annoyed.

My anger flared again.

"Oh no buddy, I paid good money to learn how to cook and I'm not going anywhere until you teach me to cook."

I picked up a mangled carrot from the table and tossed it at him. He caught it easily, confirming my suspicion that he was a shifter. They all had incredible reflexes.

"I expect better lessons than this next time too. I can't serve people vegetables that look like I pulled them out of a meat grinder."

I had no idea what his problem was, but there was no way I was going to give him an easy out.

"Fine," he ground out. "I'll see you next week then."

I stomped out, ignoring Donald in the hallway, and headed up the street to Rosewater Emporium. I knew my sisters were both there today, and I needed to be around people who didn't hate me for no reason.

When I entered the shop, I saw a woman I'd never seen before leaning on the counter next to my sister Cami.

"There she is," Cami said, pointing towards me. "That's Pepper."

The woman rushed towards me, an eager look on her pretty face.

"Pepper, hi I'm Angelica. Can I hang out with you for a while?"

Given that I'd never seen the woman before, it was a strange request.

"What? Why?"

"I need to find my mate and I heard that you're the woman to see."

I ignored Cami silently laughing behind the woman's back.

"Sorry lady, I have my own troubles today."

Charles

"Do you want to talk about what just happened?" Donald asked.

I'd been staring at the prep table ever since Pepper stormed out a couple of minutes ago. Deformed carrots and radishes sat in a sad little pile in front of me. My mate was beautiful, but she had crappy knife skills.

"No, I don't." My voice was harsh, but I didn't care. My mind was reeling from this unexpected development.

You were harsh to our mate, my inner animal reminded me angrily. *You probably hurt her feelings.*

I ignored him and turned to meet Donald's perceptive gaze. I'd met the man less than two hours ago, but I could already tell that he was a cool guy. I had a feeling that we were going to be good friends – as long as he didn't pry into my personal life.

"Pepper is your mate, huh?"

My eyes widened. I guess he was going there.

"How did you know?"

"I just went through it myself a few weeks ago. I recognized the combination of happiness, horniness, and obsession. What I don't understand is why you seem so upset about it."

"I don't want a mate," I bit out.

"Really? Because most shifters wait their whole lives to find their fated mates and some never do. The day I found Janice was the best day of my life," he said. "You're lucky, not just because you found your fated mate, but also because you got a good one. Pepper is awesome. She's smart as a whip, and funny too."

"Look, I'm a hybrid. A mix of three supernatural beings. A freak. Grown ass shifters have screamed in fear when they saw me. I can't bring that into a relationship. Also, I like being single."

"Yeah, I really liked being single until I met Janice. Now I like being mated much better."

Donald's cheerfulness was grating.

"Can we just get to work?"

He studied me for a long moment.

"How about we go for a run tonight after work?" he suggested. "You can work off that nervous energy that I'm sure is coursing through you right now, and hopefully it will clear your head so you can figure out what to do about Pepper."

My animal perked up at the invitation. I hadn't let him out in several weeks since I was busy with the move. Plus, living in New York City, shifting was always difficult. It was different here in Greysden where you could see people shift into their animals right on the street corner in broad daylight. I'd seen that exact thing happen on my way to work only this morning.

"Actually, a run sounds good. Thank you."

The rest of the day passed in a flurry of activity. When I left Wolf Kitchens I stopped by my rental to put some meat in the slow cooker, then jogged over to the spot I was supposed to meet Donald. Greysden was surrounded by acres and acres of woods, all part of the national forest, providing multiple access points for shifters to let their animals out and go for a run.

Speaking of New York, when I got to the meeting place my cousin Duncan was there, along with another man I'd never seen before. He was dressed in expensive clothes and had a bit of a snobby air about him.

Duncan walked over and gave me a one-armed hug. "Hey cousin, I hope you don't mind us crashing your run. When we ran into Donald, he invited us along."

"No problem at all," I reassured him.

Duncan introduced me to the other man. "This is my boss and friend Preston."

Ah, the guy who'd been turned into a wolf shifter a few years ago. I shook hands with the man, then we all stripped down to our skin and stashed our clothing in boxes that the town set out at all the trailheads to keep clothes and other belongings safe and dry.

I cleared my throat. "I just want to warn you guys, my animal is kind of weird."

Donald laughed, like he'd seen hybrids before. And maybe he had. "Okay then you need to shift first so we can all see this."

I closed my eyes and called forth my animal. I took a deep breath in and as I exhaled, my body morphed. Muscles lengthened and strengthened, bones cracked and reformed, and fur sprouted. I dropped to all fours as my hands and feet turned into paws, and my canines lengthened.

Duncan changed with me, since he'd already seen my animal, but Preston and Donald walked around, studying me. I had the body of a wolf, the head of a horned demon, and long vampire fangs protruding past my mouth. My front legs ended in demon claws and my back paws were wolf. I knew I looked ridiculous, like some kind of science experiment gone wrong.

To their credit, Donald and Preston just shrugged like they'd seen weirder beings, and maybe here in Greysden, they had. When they called forth their wolves without any commentary on my appearance, I exhaled in relief.

The four of us took off at a good pace, chasing each other and growling at smaller animals. Even though my animal was weird looking, I loved being in this form. All my senses were sharper now. I could smell the faintest scents in the woods, and my body moved easily across the uneven ground of the forest, running faster than I could when I was on two feet. I felt totally at ease in the woods, making me glad that I'd made the decision to move out to Colorado.

By the time we finished our run, my muscles were tired, and my mind was clearer than it had been all day. Thanking the guys for coming with me, I pulled on my clothes and headed back towards my rental. As I walked, I thought about Pepper. My mate. She was fiery. Terrible with a knife, and thank the gods for that, because if she knew how to hold one properly, I was pretty sure she would have gutted me like a fish.

My entire life, I'd felt like an outcast. A freak. As compelling as my mate was, there was no way I was going to act on my feelings. I just needed to stay far away from her until my attraction towards her faded.

Then I smelled smoke.

Pepper

I woke up cranky as hell after a night of tossing and turning in my bed. I couldn't get that rude chef guy out of my mind. There was something about Charles that was incredibly compelling, although goddess knows it wasn't his shiny personality.

Maybe it was his hands. I'd found myself staring at them during our class yesterday, admiring his long fingers and the play of muscles between his hands and forearms. In a moment of weakness last night, I imagined those hands sliding up my body...

Bad Pepper! I mentally smacked myself down. I needed to get that jerk out of my mind. And to do that, I needed coffee.

I headed downstairs, hoping that one of my parents had already brewed a pot. I hated waiting for the coffee pot to drip out enough coffee for a cup. Of course my mother could fill a coffee pot with the flick of her fingers, but I hadn't mastered that spell quite yet. I was halfway across the kitchen when I felt it: the sensation of a prickling at the back of my neck. I was not alone.

I turned and gasped. There, sitting right at my kitchen table, was Charles. He was wearing a pair of sweats that were several inches too short for him, and a tee shirt that was stretched to the breaking point across his chest. His feet were bare.

"What the hell are you doing in my kitchen?" I screeched. "And why are you wearing my father's clothes?"

He didn't answer, probably because his eyes were glued to my nipples. They were poking out to greet him through the thin tank top I'd worn to bed. I crossed my arms defensively, not used to having to worry about how I looked in my own damned house.

Before Cami and Meri moved out with their mates, I would sometimes run into Stephen or Preston in the morning, but they were so disgustingly in love with my sisters that they didn't give me or my boobs so much as a second glance.

"What. The hell. Are you. Doing here?" I demanded again.

"Peppermint Mugwort Rosewater!"

My eyes rolled so hard at my mother's use of my full name that I practically saw my own brain. My sisters and I all had weird plant-related names, but then again, our mother's name was Sage so maybe it was to be expected.

"Is that how you talk to guests in our home?"

Charles sent me a smirk that made me want to punch him in the throat.

"Guests? What are you talking about?"

"Poor Charles had a fire at his rental house last night," my mother said as she poured both of us a cup of coffee. "He lost everything."

I looked back to Charles for confirmation.

"Looks like there was a faulty wire on the slow cooker," he said with a look of resignation. "I left for a couple of hours to run in the woods and when I came back, the fire trucks were there soaking the last of my belongings."

I would have felt sorry for him if he wasn't such a jerk.

"Your parents were in the neighborhood and when they saw the fire, they offered me a place to stay."

My mother gave him an affectionate smile, as if they'd been friends for years instead of less than twelve hours.

"Why does he have to stay here?" I asked sullenly, my ego still stinging from the way he treated me yesterday.

People usually liked me. It was disconcerting to meet someone who didn't immediately want to be my best friend.

"Because we have a lot of room and that's what neighbors do," my mother said sternly. "He's staying in your grandmother's old suite in the east wing."

Rosewater Manor had two wings built out from the main section of the house. Each wing had four suites that included a bedroom, sitting room, private bathroom, and a balcony. In its early days,

Rosewater Manor had provided housing for the entire local coven and their families, but nowadays it was just Rosewaters living here. The spacious mansion gave us all a lot of privacy.

But even though Charles' suite was on the opposite side of the house, it still felt too close for me. Something about him unsettled me.

"I've got to head out to the Emporium," Mom said, squeezing our guest's shoulder as she passed by. "Please Charles, you make yourself at home. Help yourself to anything in the kitchen."

I had the oddest urge to growl at her for touching him. Mom gave me a stern look over his shoulder and mouthed, "Be nice."

Out loud she said, "I'll see you both later. Have a good day."

As soon as she was out of the room, I turned to Charles.

"I thought you had family here," I said. "Can't you stay with Duncan?"

"Would you want to be in a small house with two fated mates in a new relationship?" he asked wryly. "They could scarcely keep their paws off each other when we had dinner together the other night."

Remembering all the times that I accidentally saw or heard my sisters and their mates going at it, I couldn't help but grimace. If there was one thing the shifters loved, it was sex. "Yeah, good point."

I walked over to the cabinet and pulled out a pop-tart, heading for the toaster on the counter and popping it in one of the slots.

"What are you doing?" Charles asked.

I frowned. "Not that it's any of your business, but I'm toasting a pop tart."

"You can't eat that shit," he said. "It has no nutritional value."

"It's strawberry."

He jumped to his feet with a low growl. "I'm making you a real breakfast."

"I don't want a real breakfast. I want a pop-tart."

Ignoring me, he stuck his head into the refrigerator, returning with a handful of vegetables and a carton of eggs. He poked around the cabinets until he found everything he was looking for, then started cooking something on the stove.

When I took my pop-tart out of the toaster, he practically flew across the room and took it from my hand.

"Hey!" I said angrily. "That's mine."

"You're too old to be eating like a toddler," he said as he brushed by me and tossed my breakfast in the garbage can. I stared at him in shock. That was my last pop-tart he'd tossed in the trash, damn it.

I pointed my finger, imagining turning him into a toad like my cousin Jane had done with her ex-boyfriend once. Nothing happened. I growled in frustration.

"Who do you think you are? You don't get to tell me how to eat."

He mumbled under his breath as he returned to the stove. "I'll have breakfast for you in less than ten minutes. Trust me, you'll love it."

"Bite me."

He turned to look at me over his shoulder, his eyes burning brightly. I could see a glimmer of his animal – whatever it was – in the brown depths, and I couldn't help the shiver that slid down my spine.

"Don't tempt me."

Charles

I could feel Pepper's angry gaze practically burning through the back of my head, but I ignored her and continued cooking. Some people called me a food snob – probably because I was a food snob – but my disgust at her eating pop-tarts for breakfast was more than that. My animal had been going crazy inside me, demanding that I take care of her, and I'd been helpless to do anything else.

When I saw Pepper stumble into the kitchen half naked and rumpled from sleep, I'd almost passed out from shock. I had no idea that the nice woman who'd offered me a place to stay was Pepper's mother. My animal had been super restless ever since we got here, but I'd assumed it was just because it was freaked out from the fire.

Coming home last night to find my rental house on fire had been a blow. I'd stood there staring at the fire trucks in shock, like it wasn't real. The tiny place had gone up quickly, making me wonder if there were other electrical issues there besides the bad slow cooker. The funny thing was that I had a slow cooker of my own, but it was still in storage in New York City, so I'd used the ancient one that came with the rental. Big mistake. At least most of my stuff was still in storage so I hadn't lost much more than clothes, books, and a laptop.

Now my mate was my roommate, at least until I found a new place to rent. Despite the fact that Rosewater Manor was enormous, I could already tell that staying under the same roof as Pepper was going to make it even more difficult to stay away from her. But I needed to. I was a lone wolf. Well, a lone wolf slash demon slash vampire. I'd never even been in a long-term relationship before, and I didn't want to try one now.

She's our mate, my animal reminded me angrily. *We must claim her and make her ours.*

Ignoring my other half, I plated two servings of an egg and veggie scramble and set them on the table.

"Eat," I ordered when Pepper stayed in place with her ass leaning against the counter. She looked like she had half a mind to pull that disgusting pop-tart out of the trash.

"*Eat!*" she deepened her voice, clearly mimicking me. "Did anyone ever tell you that it's rude to order people around, especially when you're a guest in their home?"

"Nope, no one ever did."

She rolled her eyes but moved away from the counter to sit across from me at the table. I studiously kept my gaze above the neck, trying not to notice those perky tits of hers pressing against the thin fabric of her shirt. I'd been half hard since she entered the room wearing that outfit. Knowing her mother was there did nothing to help cool my lust.

I needed to find a new place to stay and do my best to keep away from Pepper until this whole mate thing blew over. But first, I needed to head into town and buy some new clothes. I couldn't go to work wearing Pepper's dad's sweatpants.

She studied her plate suspiciously, then took a cautious bite. Working with what I found in the kitchen, I'd scrambled together eggs, vegetables, fresh herbs, and cheese to make a delicious and healthy breakfast. Pepper's eyes closed in pleasure for the briefest moment. I was dying to see that expression on her face again – preferably from between her legs. She took another bite.

"How are your eggs?" I couldn't help but ask.

"Well, they're not as good as a strawberry pop tart," she said grudgingly. "But I have to admit that they are good."

I smiled around a forkful of my own breakfast. The dish was flavorful and perfectly cooked. This was another reason why it had to be a mistake that my animal thought Pepper was our fated mate. I was quite sure fate wouldn't bring me a mate who thought pop-tarts were food.

We ate the rest of our meal in silence. My animal was nagging me to talk to her the whole time, but the truth was, I didn't want to get to know her better. If I got to know her better, I'd probably start to like her. Maybe more. And I couldn't have that.

Pepper ate every bite of her food, then stood up and brought her plate to the dishwasher. Without a word, she refilled her coffee cup, then headed up the stairs. I absolutely did not watch the curves of her ass in those shorts as she headed to what I presumed was her suite of rooms.

I got through the next two days without seeing Pepper, partly because I was putting in a lot of hours at Wolf Kitchens. Donald and I were making changes to the dining room, making it look more like a high-end restaurant and less like a diner, and preparing for our grand opening in a few weeks.

Despite not seeing her in person, I could sense her in the other part of the house and so could my animal. He was becoming increasingly insistent that we find a way to spend more time with Pepper, no matter how bad of an idea it was.

My luck ran out on day three. I was at the kitchen table drinking coffee when I scented Pepper coming down the stairs a little earlier than when she usually woke up. In what I was sure was a nod to my presence in the house, she was wearing a shiny lavender robe. The robe was cinched tightly around her waist, making the thin fabric cling to every curve. Honestly, the woman could be wearing a burlap sack and I'd still get aroused looking at her.

"Good morning," I grumbled.

She looked over with a glare that made my already hardening dick lengthen. "Oh, you're still here?"

"Your mom said I could stay as long as I liked."

After doing a cursory search for rentals and finding nothing good, I decided to take Sage up on her offer to stay for a while. I wasn't quite sure if her offer was as kind as it seemed though, given the way she talked up her daughter every time I saw her. Seeing Pepper in that robe made it hard to remember why that was a problem.

"There's a frittata in the oven," I told her as she rooted around in the cabinet. She was likely looking for her new box of pop-tarts, which I'd tossed in the trash yesterday morning. When she couldn't locate them, she sent me a suspicious look.

"Where are my pop-tarts?"

I shrugged. "No clue. Eat some frittata. It's got lots of fresh vegetables, and nothing in it was made in a factory."

Pepper stalked closer, placing her hands on the table and leaning over me with a murderous look. "If I find out you took my pop-tarts, I will eviscerate you."

The air crackled around her, and the butter knife on the table lifted and started to spin before crashing back down.

"You're awfully grumpy before you've had your breakfast," I teased, to keep myself from closing the distance between us and kissing those pouty lips.

She growled in frustration, then turned to get herself some coffee and frittata. Satisfied that she was going to eat something with actual nutritional value, I stood up and put my own dishes away. I needed to get to work early today to meet with the contractors who were updating the lighting.

"I'll see you later."

She ignored me. Not that I was surprised. I couldn't help brushing against her shoulder as I left the room, gratified when I heard her sharp intake of breath. Pepper was just as affected as I was, I thought with a smile as I headed for the door. Not that either of us was going to act on it.

Sage caught me in the entryway.

"Charles, do you have a minute?"

I gave Pepper's mom a friendly smile. I really liked the older witch. "Yeah, I was just on my way to work."

"We're having a barbeque tomorrow afternoon at two. I would love for you to come."

"Um, well…"

"I know you're not working," she pressed on. "Donald will be there with Janice, and my daughters Cami and Meri are coming with their mates. Oh, and Pepper will be there of course. It'll be a good opportunity for you two to talk."

"You might not know this Sage, but Pepper doesn't like me very much. I don't want to make her uncomfortable."

She moved closer, her perceptive eyes studying me.

"You realize that my husband is a psychic, right?"

I nodded. "Yeah, I did hear that somewhere."

The town of Greysden traded gossip like it was currency. You couldn't go anywhere around here without hearing some gossip about your neighbors. I'd heard several stories about how Edward had used his psychic skills to find things that were lost, like wallets and children.

"We know the truth, Charles. Edward had a vision that Pepper is your fated mate."

My heart thudded painfully in my chest.

"What we don't know is why you're fighting it. But that's okay, you clearly need some time to adjust to the idea, especially since Pepper is fighting it too. She doesn't feel it as strongly as you do as a shifter, but she definitely feels something. The mate bond is very powerful, and you won't be able to stay away from each other forever. Fate doesn't work that way."

"I. Uh." I didn't know how to respond to this revelation.

She patted my shoulder. "You will come and eat barbecue and have a nice afternoon with your mate and her family. Maybe you and Pepper can try to get to know each other a little better."

Yes, yes, let's do that! my animal practically screamed inside me.

Sage smiled as if she could hear it. "See you tomorrow."

Pepper

I was knee deep in a design project when I heard a knock on the door to my suite. When I didn't respond immediately, the knock came again, harder this time.

"What?"

The hair on the back of my neck prickled as the handle turned and Charles stuck his head inside. I hadn't seen him since our run-in in the kitchen yesterday morning, but he hadn't been far from my mind. That frittata had been delicious, but I still couldn't figure out what he'd done with my new box of pop-tarts. I made a mental note to ask my mother to teach me how to do location spells.

"I didn't say you could come in," I snapped.

"Your mother sent me up to get you," he explained as he stepped inside. "She said to tell you it's time for dinner."

I'd been so wrapped up in my latest project that I'd almost forgotten that my parents were hosting a family and friends barbecue today. Mom loved nothing more than having a bunch of people over to Rosewater Manor so she could ply them with food while my father created elaborate cocktails for the occasion.

"Fine, tell her that I'll be down in a few minutes."

When he just stood there in the doorway, I shot him an annoyed look. He was dressed more casually than I'd ever seen him today, wearing faded jeans and a plain grey tee shirt that pulled across his muscular torso in a way that I couldn't say I hated. His hair was styled with gel though, something I definitely hated.

"Is there anything else?" I asked pointedly.

"I don't know if you've noticed, but I think your mother is trying to fix us up."

I saved my file and got up from my desk. "No shit, Sherlock."

Every time I'd seen my mother the last few days, she'd been singing the praises of our guest. It wasn't like my mother to meddle in my personal life, but she'd definitely been fixated on the idea of me getting together with Charles. Apparently one night he cooked dinner for her and my father, sealing his place on her 'most favorite projects' list.

My mother was forever taking in strays. Ever since my grandmother died, the suite where Charles was staying had been a never-ending parade of orphans, new friends, and people who needed to get away from life. Charles was the latest project, but he was more than that. My mother wanted him to be her newest son-in-law, and no amount of protesting that I hated the guy could deter her.

"Just so you know, I'm not interested in being fixed up with you." His handsome face was set in that haughty expression that put my teeth on edge.

I slammed my hands on my hips. "What makes you think I am interested in you being fixed up with me?"

I couldn't believe how arrogant this guy was. I nodded towards the door. "You can leave now."

Instead of leaving, he walked closer. I could smell an intriguing scent, it was pine and a hint of something that I could swear was butter.

"I'm sure that you're nice, but I'm not looking for a relationship right now," he continued. For some reason it sounded like he was trying to convince himself as much as me.

"Again. I am not interested in you either. Not at all."

It was almost the truth. Well, mostly the truth. My body was interested in his body, but my mind knew better.

When he continued to stare at me with those dark eyes, I put my hands on his chest and gave him a little shove. I needed to get him out of my space. Unfortunately, he was built like a wall and didn't budge at all, leaving my hands splayed across his pecs. Mmm, they were nice and hard...

A strong current of electricity singed my palms, but somehow, I couldn't move them. It was like I was frozen in place. Charles stared down at my hands, looking confused, then looked back up at me. This time when our eyes met, I could see his animal glimmering in the brown depths.

My breath caught in my throat and a flood of arousal raced through my core. His nostrils flared and I realized from the glimmer of satisfaction that crossed his face that he could smell it. Damn shifters and their super smelling abilities.

Charles stepped forward, closing the distance between us, and lifted his hands to my shoulders. His face looked almost tortured.

"I...I have to know..."

Whatever he was going to say was cut off by his lips crashing against mine. My hands fisted his shirt as he thrust his tongue into my mouth, sliding it against mine as we battled for control. The kiss turned rough as we took out our anger and aggression on each other's lips. My hands slid from his chest to his back, pulling him closer, and he pressed up against me, my curves flattened against the hardness of his body.

When I felt a certain part of his body growing harder as well, I came to my senses. What the hell? I didn't even like this guy. What was he doing to me?

I stepped back, breathing heavily, and I pressed my hands to my lips like it would erase the memory of that incredible kiss. I pointed at the door. "Leave."

When he didn't budge, I muttered a spell that made the door fly open. "Leave. Now."

Without another word, he strode out of the room, leaving me standing there wondering what had just happened. I refused to let myself think about how incredible that kiss was, and how much I wished it could happen again. Because it couldn't happen again. It had been a mistake, nothing else.

I spent the entire evening trying my best to avoid Charles, and he seemed just as determined to stay away from me despite my mother's ridiculously obvious attempts at matchmaking. I stayed on one side of the yard, talking with my sisters and my friend Janice, while Charles sat at the picnic table talking to my father, Donald, and a couple of guys who lived up the road from us.

"What's the story with that Charles guy?" my sister Cami asked me. "Mom said he's staying here now."

I shrugged. "He's the director of that new culinary kitchen, and Duncan's cousin. I guess his rental house burned down."

"How did that happen?"

"Mom said it was a kitchen fire."

Cami laughed. "The chef burned down his kitchen? That's weird." Her eyes traveled across the yard again and then back to me. "He is super hot though."

I heard a growl and Stephen came racing over to sit at my sister's feet on the grass. Reaching over, I patted him on the head.

"Good dog, protecting my sister from that big bad chef."

Stephen rolled his eyes, then leaned back against Cami's legs as if he couldn't bear to not be touching her.

"Why don't you just pee on me and get it over with?" Cami asked in exasperation. "The guy's a shifter, he can tell I'm mated."

"But he's not mated yet," Stephen responded.

Just then my mother walked by. "He will be soon, don't worry."

Then she looked right at me and gave me a smile.

Charles

I bit my lip to keep from growling as I saw Pepper pat Stephen on the head. I knew the guy was mated to her sister, but my animal did not like seeing her touch another male, no matter how innocent it was. He was pushing at me, insisting that I grab Pepper, bring her back to our den, and officially make her our mate. Now that we'd tasted her, he was not going to rest until she was wearing our claiming mark on her body.

My insistence that it wasn't going to happen meant nothing.

My mind returned to that kiss we'd shared earlier. It had been short, barely a couple of minutes, yet it was burned into my memory. The feel of her soft curves against my body, the taste of her lips, it had been too much to process. I already knew that no matter what happened with Pepper, I'd never be able to kiss another female after that.

I was grateful that she'd come to her senses and pulled away, because I'd been too far gone to think clearly. A few more minutes and I would have been rutting into her like the beast that I was.

"So, you and Pepper, huh?"

I glanced over at Preston, the CEO who I'd met on the run the night of the fire. He was a nice guy, typical of the rich New York City men I was used to interacting with. He and the quirky psychic Meri made an odd couple, but from what I could tell, they were totally besotted with each other.

"It's not like that," I protested.

"Really? Because I might have only been a wolf for a couple of years, but I know the look of someone watching their mate." He glanced between us again. "You need to mark her, man. Your animal won't rest until you've locked her down."

"I'm not looking for a mate," I said quietly.

"Looks like you found one though," he said.

"Even if I did want a mate, it wouldn't work. Pepper hates me."

Preston laughed. "Meri hated me at first too. That fiery hatred makes it all the more satisfying when you finally get to mark her."

Preston's words ran on repeat in my brain for the rest of the weekend.

I managed to avoid Pepper, but when I headed into Wolf Kitchens on Monday, I knew I was going to have to face her again. She'd been clear last week that she had no intention of dropping the cooking class. I just needed to minimize contact outside of class. Oh, and find a new place to live. I'd been dragging my feet on that, and I couldn't explain why.

I pulled in Donald to help with the lessons, and once our students were settled at their stations, I began a lesson about roasting. It was a simple technique that worked for things like vegetables and chicken, thus making it an easy thing to handle for beginners.

Except Pepper. Despite our knife lessons last week, she struggled to prepare her vegetables, nearly slicing off a finger in the process of cutting a carrot. Donald went to help her, but when he reached around her to show her an easier way to cut the carrot, my animal went crazy. Before I knew what was happening, I'd strode across the room and shoved Donald away from her with a growl.

My friend sent me a knowing smirk and moved onto another student as I took his place at Pepper's back. She stiffened immediately. This close I could smell her shampoo, something citrusy. She'd pulled her hair up today, but several long strands had already escaped confinement to hang around her neck and face. A single drop of sweat slid down the side of her face, and it took everything in me not to lick it off her skin.

"Like this," I said quietly, bending her fingers with my own. "Keep the knife away from your fingertips, and hold it near the blade like this, not at the end of the handle."

"I'd like to use the knife on something else," she muttered under her breath.

I couldn't help but smile at her feistiness.

When Pepper got the hang of cutting, I stepped back, keeping a watchful eye on her while walking around the classroom. We finished prepping the chicken and vegetables, then moved onto the actual cooking. The class was a mix of young people and retirees, with Pepper the only student between the ages of twenty-five and sixty-five.

While the food cooked, we made a simple fruit salad to spoon over sponge cake for dessert. The room filled with the delicious scent of roasted chicken, making my stomach growl.

"Hungry?" Donald asked.

Reluctantly I took my gaze off Pepper. "I didn't have breakfast today."

I didn't share that I'd been too chickenshit to go into the kitchen in case I ran into Pepper wearing her clingy robe.

My friend laughed and clapped me on the shoulder. "I wasn't talking about food, my friend."

I heard Pepper groan in frustration, and hurried over to see what the problem was, despite my resolution to stay away from her.

"It's not cooked through," she explained.

At first I thought there was an issue with the oven, but then I realized it was human error.

"You only turned the oven to two twenty-five," I told her. "It was supposed to be four twenty-five."

She huffed in frustration, then waved her finger at the half-cooked chicken.

"*Coque!*" she said firmly. "*Calidum!*"

The chicken heated before our eyes, then split apart and burst into flames. I wrapped my arm around Pepper's waist, pulling her to safety as Donald rushed over and covered the flaming chicken with the lid of a roasting pan to put out the fire.

"Damn it," Pepper said sadly. "I can't cook OR do magic right."

"You're perfect just the way you are," I whispered.

I gave her a brief squeeze, then stepped away before I got any crazy ideas, like leaning her over the cooking table and taking her from behind.

It was a relief when the class was finally over and Pepper filed out of the room with the rest of the students. Donald and I lingered afterward, cleaning up the space.

"You can't fight this forever," Donald called from the other side of the room.

I didn't even pretend to not know what he was talking about. "Sure I can."

Donald shook his head. "You're a stubborn one, I'll give you that. But sooner or later your animal is going to take over and you won't have a choice but to claim your mate."

The rest of the day passed quickly. Donald and I continued to work with the contractors to update the dining room while the kitchen staff ran through some of the new menu items. We were hoping to open the restaurant by the end of the month if things continued to go smoothly. I couldn't wait. I loved the frenetic energy of a busy restaurant.

I'd fallen in love with cooking as a child. My demon grandmother had taught me all of her recipes, and before long I was cooking for my family. My mother was a disaster in the kitchen – much like my mate—and I was glad to take over the cooking duties at an early age. My grandmother died years ago but I could still picture her standing over the stove, a spoon in her hand, telling me that someday I was going to make a woman very happy by cooking for her.

Little did I know that woman who fate chose for me would prefer pop-tarts to cooking.

Pepper

"This is pointless. I'm never going to get it."

Meri looked up from her book with a frown. We'd gone down to the lake to practice spell craft, with Meri quizzing me like we were prepping for the SATs or something.

"The problem is that you're distracted, Peppermint. You need to empty your mind and focus on your magic."

"How do you know?" I snipped. "You're not a witch."

"No, but I learned a thing or two growing up in a house full of them," she reminded me. "Now focus on making that flower bloom."

I closed my eyes and consciously pushed all other thoughts out of my mind. When I opened my eyes again, I focused on the plant stem, visualizing it bending to my will and growing a bloom. Slowly a bud appeared, and soft petals began to grow out, spreading into a flower. I resisted celebrating, instead staying focused on the bright yellow flower.

Suddenly I heard a fierce growl, followed by rustling. The noise broke my attention, and the flower wilted, the petals falling to the ground.

"Damn it," I muttered.

I looked around to see what the noise was, and something came charging out of the woods heading right towards me.

"What the hell?"

The animal was like nothing I'd ever seen before. Its body looked like a giant wolf, but it had the head and horns of a demon with two long pointed fangs protruding from its mouth. Its front feet looked like cloven hooves while its back feet were wolf paws. Clearly it was a shifter, I just wasn't sure what kind.

The animal skidded to a stop next to me, watching me carefully.

"What is that?" Meri asked. "It looks like a monster from a children's book."

For some reason I had the sense that she was hurting the creature's feelings with her words.

"I think he's cute. Aren't you just the cutest thing?" I cooed, rubbing the top of his head between his horns. He was cute, in a mutt kind of way.

The animal leaned against my leg, making a soft chuffing noise as I slipped my hands into the soft fur of its torso and rubbed up and down its spine. The beast seemed familiar for some reason.

My sister gasped.

"Oh my goddess, Pepper!" Meri walked over, staring at the creature. "This was in one of my visions a while back. The day we reversed Cami's love spell I had a vision that your mate was a monster, remember?"

I looked at my sister in surprise. "This is what, um who, you saw?"

She nodded vigorously. "Yesh, it's him. This monster is your mate."

"He's not a monster, he's some kind of hybrid like Gabe," I told her, referring to our cousin Jane's mate, who was a wolf demon hybrid.

I glanced down into the creature's dark eyes and suddenly I knew exactly who this was.

"Charles? Is that you?"

The creature nodded his head, and I could swear he looked vulnerable. A flood of conflicting emotions rushed through me.

"Meri."

"Yeah?" my sister asked.

"Go away."

"You got it."

My sister took off, a wide smile on her face, and once she was out of earshot I said, "You might as well change back to human so we can talk."

The air around the creature shimmered, and soon the human side of Charles appeared, crouching on the ground. As he pushed to standing, I realized that he was naked. Of course, he was naked. It wasn't like his clothes shifted with him.

"Is it true?" I asked, carefully keeping my eyes on his face. "We're fated mates?"

Charles nodded. "Yeah. It's true."

That explained the strong pull I felt towards him, despite his obnoxious personality. It also explained why he kept invading my dreams, especially after we kissed in my room last weekend.

"That's why you said 'not her' when you met me, isn't it? You realized I was your mate, and you were rejecting me."

"Yeah," he said again. He looked miserable.

I felt a rush of pain that nearly took my breath away.

"Okay, good to know." My voice was cold as ice.

I moved around him and started walking back towards our house. I couldn't decide if I was hurt or angry. It figured that when I found my mate, he'd be some jerk who didn't even want me. Maybe he thought he was too good to have a mate like me.

"It's your loss, buddy. I would be a kick ass mate."

"Wait," he called. "Pepper, we should talk."

I turned around and gave him my best glare.

"The time to talk was when you realized I was your mate. You don't want me. I get it. No hard feelings because you're not who I would choose either. How about we forget this whole conversation and continue avoiding each other as much as possible until you find your own place?"

Pain crossed his face. "No. I mean, well, I don't know what I mean."

"That's helpful," I sighed, turning again. I needed to get home.

I heard Charles starting to follow me so I turned, sending up a thick cloud of dirt in his path with a gesture from my hand.

"*Tempestus!*" The dirt swirled like a tornado, blocking his path. I heard Charles coughing on the other side of the wall of dirt. I gave myself an internal fist bump for getting that spell to work so well on the fly.

"Pepper!" Charles coughed as he got a mouthful of flying dirt.

"Leave me alone."

I ran back through the woods to my house. It was a bad idea to run away from a predator, but I just wanted to be alone to lick my wounds. I needed time to think about what I'd learned and process the rejection. After a few minutes I heard Charles running up behind me. I had a good head start, and he didn't catch up to me, fortunately for his balls.

Bursting through the back door of our house, I ignored Meri and my mother chatting at the kitchen table and pounded up the stairs to my suite. I didn't realize that Charles was still behind me until I heard the stairs creaking under his weight. Putting on speed, I dashed for my door, intending to slam it in his arrogant face, but he got there in the nick of time, pushing his palm against the door.

"Go. Away." I threw my weight against the door, but it wouldn't budge.

"Please, Pepper, let me explain."

"There's nothing to explain," I said, throwing myself against the door again. "You don't like me, I don't like you, so we'll just wait for the fated mate thing to go away."

He sighed deeply, then pushed the door open enough to slide through the opening at the same time I threw myself against the wood again. My forward momentum slammed the door behind him, leaving us alone in the sitting room.

I turned around to face him, chest heaving. Charles reached out his hand, then lowered it again.

"It wasn't you, Pepper. It's me."

Charles

"Yeah, I've used that line many times before, I get it."

Pepper stalked across the room angrily, heading toward the bedroom.

"My whole life I wanted a mate," she said, almost to herself. "I watched my sisters, my friends, and random people on the street find their mates and I tried to be hopeful. But I guess I should have given up long ago. I'm destined to rattle around this big old house with a bunch of cats. Not that I even like cats that much. Maybe I can get a bird or something."

"Pepper."

She startled, almost as if she'd forgotten that I was there. I stalked across the room, grabbing her wrist.

"Please, can we just sit down and talk for a few minutes?"

When I tugged her towards the small couch, she dug in her heels. She might have been smaller than me, but my mate was strong.

"You're not going to sit your naked ass on my couch," she screeched. "Go put on some pants."

I knew instinctively that she was not going to let me in again if I left, so instead I headed into the bathroom and grabbed a towel from the cabinet, wrapping it around my waist.

I sat on the couch, and Pepper reluctantly sat across from me, as far away as she could possibly be.

"The thing is, I've always felt like a freak," I started, my throat feeling suddenly tight. "Like your sister said, I was looked at as a monster. I grew up being teased. I never fit in anywhere. I wasn't like the shifters, I wasn't like the demons, and I sure wasn't like those snobby vampires. To make things worse, the mixed nature of my animal made him hard to control when I was younger, and we didn't even know another hybrid who could help me."

I took a deep breath. Talking about my childhood as a misfit was painful, even now.

"While the other supernatural kids were going for runs together and playing video games and kicking human ass in sports, I was in the kitchen with my grandmother, creating recipes. Being in the kitchen, cooking and baking, it was the one thing I was good at, the one place where I didn't feel like an outsider. I decided that I would never have a mate, that no one would want a hybrid freak like me, and that was okay."

Pepper was watching me closely now, her expression soft with sympathy.

"Once I turned forty, my mother had enough. She wanted me to settle down and give her some little hybrid grandkids, so she started trying to fix me up with random females, and that just solidified my desire to stay single."

I repressed a shudder as I remembered the calculating female I'd discovered in my bed right before I decided to apply for the job in Greysden.

"Why are you telling me this?" Pepper asked.

"I want you to understand why I acted like I did. Why I freaked out when I realized that you were my mate."

"Fine, thank you for sharing. You can go now."

Hurt and anger warred for dominance on her face as she crossed her arms under her breasts and stared me down. With everyone else, Pepper tended to be lighthearted and jokey, but around me she got that stern look which made me excited every single time.

"You liked my animal," I said softly. I still couldn't believe it.

"What?"

"Your sister called me a monster, and you defended me," I reminded her. "You didn't cringe in fear or revulsion when you saw me running toward you. You even petted me. It made me realize that maybe all these years I was wrong about not being able to find a woman who could accept me like I am."

I scooted across the cushion so I could be closer to her.

"When you petted me and called me cute, it made me realize that my animal is right. You belong to me."

"I don't belong to anyone," she protested.

"You will, mate." It felt good to finally use the word.

I gripped her waist, picking her up and swinging her around until she straddled my lap. Her eyes widened in surprise at the move.

"What are you doing?" she asked breathlessly.

"This."

I cupped the back of her head with one hand and used the other to draw her closer. When our lips were only a few inches apart I paused, waiting to see if she was going to pull away from me. Hoping that she wouldn't. She swayed towards me, and it broke the last of my control.

My lips crashed against hers in a rough kiss that immediately set my entire body on fire with desire.

Yes, my animal cheered. *Mark her! Claim our mate!*

I nipped at her lower lip until she granted me entrance to the sweet heat of her mouth. My tongue tangled with Pepper's while my free hand moved to her hip, sliding her closer to me.

Pepper gripped my shoulders and tilted her head to give me better access. The towel fell away from my waist as she ground her pelvis against mine, making my cock harden and swell more than I thought was possible.

"Pepper. Mate."

My chest was heaving when we finally pulled apart, and I couldn't help but lick my way down her neck, paying special attention to the spot where I planned to mark her. But when I caught her skin between my teeth, she pushed back.

"No marking," she said firmly. "I'm not sure if I like you yet, I'm not ready to commit."

I rolled my cock against the apex of her legs, and she groaned.

"You like me fine right there," I said as I inhaled the scent of her arousal.

"Are you going to bore me with the sound of your voice or fuck me?" she asked irritably.

"Fuck you, definitely fuck you."

"Then shut up and do it," she said.

My jaw dropped as she ripped her shirt off, sending it sailing across the room with her bra right behind it. Her breasts were full and round, pale skin offset by dark pink nipples that seemed to be pointed right at me.

Pepper gripped my face, closing her lips over mine, and this time she was the aggressor. I leaned back, content to let her take the lead as she kissed me and ran her palms over my chest and shoulders. My hands curled into fists as I fought for control. When I couldn't take it any longer, I pressed one hand against her chest.

"On your hands and knees," I ordered.

I thought she'd fight me, but instead she rolled off my lap and knelt on the couch, her hands gripping the armrest. I moved behind her, kissing my way down her back and then up again. I pulled off her jeans, taking her panties with them, and maneuvered her out of them in record time.

My eyes widened as I revealed the pale globes of her ass. My mate was perfect for me, soft and curvy. Unable to resist, I pressed my lips against her skin on one side, and then the other, until Pepper made a sound of impatience. Then I lowered over her back, surrounding her with my body.

"I want you," I whispered in her ear. Then I gave it a little nip with my teeth, and she groaned loudly.

"Charles. Please."

It was the consent I needed. I shifted positions and, gripping her ass cheeks firmly, I lined my cock up with her opening and sunk deeply into her heat. We both groaned as I bottomed out, my pelvis connecting with her ass. She squeezed me so tight I could barely breathe. I stayed completely still, wanting to savor the moment, but Pepper pushed back against me.

"Move!" she ordered.

And I did.

Pepper

It felt like Charles was splitting me in two as he pounded into me, but I loved it. I loved the burning stretch of my pussy around his cock. I loved the way the force of his thrusts pushed me against the arm of the couch. I loved the way he whispered filthy yet oddly sweet words of endearment in my ear.

Sleeping with this man was probably a terrible idea, but right now I couldn't remember why that was.

"I need you to come," he groaned against my shoulder. "I don't know how long I'm going to last. I want you too much."

The girl in me was thrilled. I'd enjoyed a healthy sex life over the years, but no one had ever wanted me so badly that they had to fight for control. And no man had made me so close to coming with only a few thrusts of his hips.

I squeezed my internal muscles against him, making him growl. Charles shifted positions, moving his hands around my body to pull and pinch at my nipples. The combination of pain and pleasure was enough for me to lose control, gasping as my orgasm rolled through my body.

"Charles!" His name came out as a high-pitched wail.

"I'm right here, mate. I've got you."

He fucked me through my orgasm, and when I was done, he continued pounding into me while circling my clit with his thumb. I'd never been a multiple orgasm kind of woman, but damned if that thumb didn't send me right over the edge into a second orgasm, this one longer and stronger than the first one.

I shook beneath him, my vision turning fuzzy as waves of release rolled through me.

Behind me, Charles' movements became erratic. He shoved into me roughly, paused, then shoved in again, this time releasing a stream of his cum deep inside me. Pulling back, he groaned, then pushed back in again to release more of his seed.

"Mate!"

Charles lowered his mouth to the juncture of my shoulder and my neck, nipping my skin as he shook around me.

"No marking," I reminded him.

He sighed deeply, then collapsed on top of me, pushing me flat on the couch as he landed on my back.

"Fuck," he whispered.

"You're squishing me," I complained. The guy weighed a ton.

Charles rolled off me but ran out of couch, landing on the floor with a loud thump. "We need to do this in a bed next time," he groused.

"There's going to be a next time?" I teased. "That's pretty bold."

He leapt to his feet with the natural grace of his shifter side, grabbing me off the couch and carrying me into the bedroom bridal style. I landed on the bed with a little bounce, and Charles stretched himself over me. He wasn't as bulky as a lot of shifters, but he was still wide and solid, his skin stretched over hard muscles.

If he noticed the softness of my belly or the slight sagging of my breasts, he didn't say anything. I wasn't in my twenties anymore, hell I was nearly forty, and things had shifted with time and gravity.

"There's going to be a forever of next times," he said, answering my earlier question.

I still wasn't sure how I felt about the mate thing, but my body was humming beneath his, begging for more, and I wasn't going to argue with that right now. Instead, I wrapped my legs around his waist, making his cock slip between my folds.

"Less talking, more fucking," I ordered.

We spent the rest of the afternoon and evening in bed, making each other come over and over until we were both exhausted, dehydrated, and covered with sweat.

I was wishing that I was the kind of witch who could conjure up food and water out of thin air when I heard a knock on the outer door of the suite.

"I'm leaving you two a tray," I heard my mother call cheerfully. "In case you need to refuel."

My face burned with embarrassment as I realized that my mother, and probably the rest of my family, knew what we were doing up here. Charles appeared completely unbothered. He levered himself off the bed and returned two minutes later with a tray laden down with covered plates of food, two bottles of beer, four water bottles, and an entire package of Oreo cookies.

I went right for the cookies, squealing when Charles tried to grab them out of my hand.

"I'm an adult, I can eat dessert first," I told him as I defiantly bit into a cookie.

He rolled his eyes, and I leaned forward, shoving one into his mouth. "Eat."

He chewed thoughtfully. "This is pretty good."

"You've never had an Oreo?" I asked incredulously.

He shook his head. "My mother didn't allow junk food in the house when we were growing up."

"Well, you really missed out, my friend. Oreos are an American institution. A giant among cookies."

I lifted the lid off one of the plates, revealing a stack of grilled cheese and tomato sandwiches, my mother's favorite comfort food. Another plate had cut vegetables and a container of hummus. Two small bags of potato chips were tucked between the dishes, along with two bananas.

I bit into a grilled cheese sandwich happily. "Yum! You've got to try this. Mom uses four different kinds of cheese."

We leaned against the headboard, tucking into our meal with enthusiasm. As we ate, for the first time in our relationship we talked, really talked. It was nice. When Charles wasn't acting like he had a stick up his ass, he was charming and thoughtful with a dry sense of humor.

I couldn't help but feel sympathy for the way he'd grown up thinking his hybrid animal was a freak. Growing up thinking I was the only normal in a family of magical beings, I was well acquainted with the experience of never quite fitting in, even with your own family. It gave me a unique insight into his personality.

After we ate our meal, we shared a shower and fell into an exhausted sleep. Somewhere in the middle of the night I started to think that maybe this mate thing would work out okay after all. Then I woke up in the morning alone.

Charles

I was just about to walk into work when my phone rang. My mother's picture popped up on the screen and I wondered if she had someone spying on me here or something. It was the only explanation for the way she opened the call, not even pausing to say hello.

"You found your mate?" she shrieked.

I looked around, but the streets were mostly empty. Greysden didn't really start waking up until after nine in the morning.

"Hi Ma, I'm fine thanks for asking."

"Don't 'hi Ma' me, I can't believe I had to hear about your new mate from Joyce Hendricks."

"Who's Joyce Hendricks?" I asked in confusion.

"She's the sister-in-law of Elana Jerguson, who heard from her daughter that her partner's friend who is friends with your cousin Duncan's mate told her that you found your mate."

I rubbed my temples. It was way too early to track all that. I wasn't sure how Duncan knew about us unless Preston told him. Yeah, that had to be it. The last time I saw Duncan was the night before I met Pepper.

"I'm not sure if that female is really my mate," I lied.

I couldn't say why I said it other than I wasn't in the mood to answer a bunch of questions from my mother, especially about a woman who refused to let me mark her as my mate. Pepper's reticence stung, especially after the incredible night we'd shared.

"Does your animal say she's your mate?"

"Yeah," I admitted.

"Quit messing around, Charles Maximillan Fields. You know how this works, if your animal says she's your mate, she's your mate. Now, when do I get to meet this girl?"

"It's complicated, Ma."

"What's complicated about it, Charles? You find your fated mate, you mark her, then you make me the grandchildren I've been waiting for all these years." She paused. "Ooh, maybe you've already gotten her pregnant. That would be awesome. Does she seem pregnant? Has her smell changes?"

"No Ma, she's not pregnant." At least I didn't think she was. "Besides, I don't want a mate, remember?"

"Too bad, you've got one now."

"I'm not even sure that she likes me," I admitted.

"What?" My mother's screech made my head pound more. "I'm going to come talk to this woman who thinks she's too good to be my son's mate."

"No, Ma, please don't come here. We got off to a rocky start, but I'm working on it. You can come visit once everything gets settled, and then you can meet her. I promise."

I was still reeling from the events of the last twenty-four hours. The instant that Pepper stroked my fur and said I was cute, I was a goner. The fact that she could look past the fact that my animal looked like some kind of a science experiment gone wrong told me everything I needed to know. Pepper was the woman for me. My soulmate.

I told you, my animal reminded me. He then went into an extended rant about how I'd spent hours in her bed and avoided marking her. Reminding my animal side that Pepper had forbidden it did nothing to calm him down. He thought I should have ignored her and done it anyway. Now he was edgy and irritable having her out of our sight and not wearing a mate mark.

When I walked inside the restaurant there was a crew there refinishing the floors. It was the last cosmetic change we were making before we officially opened. The dining room had gone from looking like a small-town diner to a reasonably nice restaurant, and I was itching to get some customers in here to try our newly imagined menu.

Once the restaurant was running smoothly, our next project was opening the culinary training program.

"We should do a soft opening next week," I told Donald as we watched the kitchen crew make lunch for the guys working on the floors. "Only for family and friends."

"Good idea," my head chef said. "It will help us work out any kinks in our service."

I made a mental note to send out invitations to people we knew and trusted. Unbidden, the image of Pepper and I eating dinner in the corner came to my mind. I sighed. I used to be a guy who could focus one hundred percent on his career, but ever since Pepper came into my life, she seemed to push into my thoughts on a regular basis.

"How's it going with Pepper?" Donald asked, as if he'd read my mind.

"Um, okay."

There must have been something in my face because my friend slapped me on the shoulder with a wide smile.

"You finally mated her? Good job!"

"Not exactly," I said, feeling a flush rise up my face. I wasn't the kind of person who shared my problems with anyone, but I could use some advice. Charles had recently found his mate, maybe he could help me with my own mate issues.

"Did uh, Janice have a problem with you marking her?" I asked. "Like, was she hesitant or something?"

"Are you kidding? She was sinking her teeth into my neck before I even unzipped my pants the first time."

His face turned sympathetic. "Oh, wait, are you saying that Pepper won't let you mark her?"

"No. She is quite adamant that I not mark her, but I don't understand why."

"That's so weird. Janice told me that as long as she's known Pepper, she's wanted to fall in love and have a mate. She even had her sister whip up a love potion to try to move things along one time." Donald chuckled. "Of course, the spell went a little sideways and Cami summoned her own mate instead."

"They seem happy enough," I said, remembering how snuggly Stephen and Cami were at the barbecue the other day.

"Yeah, since they worked things out, they've been inseparable."

"I don't know what to do," I said miserably. "I know I hurt her by rejecting her initially, but once we um, got closer to each other in the intimate sense, I thought she'd get over it and accept a mating. I want to spend the rest of my life with her. I love her, man."

"With a woman as strong willed as Pepper, you're going to have to play dirty," Donald said. "Tease her. Torture her. Don't give her what she wants until she gives you what you want."

"I don't know if I can do that."

Now that I knew what it felt like to be inside my mate, I didn't think that I'd have the patience to keep her at arm's length. I wasn't one to play games, but then again, if I kept sleeping with her, there was a good chance I'd never get a commitment.

My phone buzzed in my pocket, and I pulled it out to find yet another text from my mother demanding to hear more about my mate. She hadn't been happy when I'd cut off our call earlier.

"I guess if worse comes to worse, I can sic my mother on her."

Pepper

When I came into the kitchen the next morning, Charles was sitting at the kitchen table, sipping a cup of coffee. He was bare chested, wearing only low-slung pajama bottoms. My pussy clenched needily. I thought for sure he'd come up to my suite last night when he got home from work, but he hadn't.

I'd spent much of the night alternating between wondering what I'd done to push him away and getting irritated that he'd gotten me into bed and then ghosted me.

"Hey."

"Good morning, Pepper."

He gave me a hot look, his eyes traveling slowly from my face to my breasts and down to my toes before coming back up again. His gaze was like a caress, and my body responded immediately. His nostrils flared as he took notice.

"Sit down. I made breakfast."

I was so discombobulated that I complied with his growled order. He brought me a cup of coffee, his bare arm sliding against mine after he set the cup down.

"I'll be back with a plate," he whispered in my ear. I shivered.

He returned with a plate of cottage cheese with fruit, sausage, and a large square pastry perfectly centered on the plate, a paper doily beneath it.

"What is this?" I asked, poking it with my fork.

"It's a homemade strawberry pop-tart."

My eyes flew to his. "You know how to make pop-tarts?" I asked excitedly. "Why have you been holding out on me?"

"Eat your breakfast."

He sat across from me, watching me as I tried the pop-tart.

"Holy crap," I groaned as an explosion of flavor hit my tongue. "This tastes really good."

"It's not the only thing that tastes good," he said, his eyes lowering as if he could see my pussy through the tabletop.

I gulped around my fork. Charles continued to watch me as I ate my breakfast, and somehow it was one of the most erotic things that had ever happened to me.

But still, there was this weird distance between us. I wanted to ask him why he'd left my bed without a word yesterday morning, and why I hadn't seen him since, but I didn't want to be that needy girl who forced 'where is this going' conversations on guys. I thought things were solid between us what with the mate thing and the sixteen-hour sex-a-thon, but I guessed I was wrong. Maybe after he slept with me Charles realized that his animal was wrong about us being mates.

I swallowed a stab of hurt. I didn't even really like him that much, I consoled myself, although I liked him more now than I did a few days ago. If Charles and I weren't fated mates it was better that we called things off now before I did something stupid, like falling in love with the guy.

Reminding myself that I had a lot of work to do for my clients, I finished my breakfast and took my dishes over to the dishwasher.

"Thanks for breakfast," I called over my shoulder. "The pop-tart was delicious."

I would never in a million years admit this, but it was better than the kind that came in a box.

"You're quite welcome," he said.

I jumped as I realized that Charles was right behind me. When I turned, he put his hands on either side of my body, trapping me between him and the counter. He lowered his face, nipping along my neck until I grabbed his head and pulled him up to my lips. Our kiss was rough and hot, tongues tangling as our bodies did the same. When he finally pulled back, I was gasping for breath and my panties were soaking. He stepped away from me and it took everything in me not to reach for him again.

He gave me a casual smile. "Have a good day."

I frowned in confusion. "Um, wait. Do you want to come to my room tonight?"

"I don't think that's a good idea." For some reason he wouldn't meet my eyes.

"I thought I was your mate?" I asked, hating the needy tone in my voice. "Doesn't that mean we should spend time together?"

"You are my mate, but you clearly need more time to accept it fully and make a commitment. I'll wait for you to get there."

Then he turned on his heel and stalked out of the room. I took off after him, grabbing his arm to pull him to a stop.

"You were fine with waiting to mark me when you were fucking me five times in a row," I snapped angrily.

"Six," he reminded me. "But I felt kind of cheap afterwards when I did the walk of shame back to my own room. I won't let you use me for sex."

"You're ridiculous," I said. "You spend two weeks avoiding me and being rude whenever we're together, then I pet you on the head and let you fuck me, and all the sudden I'm supposed to just lay down and let you mark me? You don't get to be hurt that I want some time to get used to the idea of us spending the rest of our lives together. I'm a human you know, well mostly human, I can't just switch on my emotions like that."

He grabbed my shoulders, staring intently into my eyes. "That's why I told you I'd wait for you to catch up, Pepper."

"And how is that going to work, exactly?" I asked.

"Let's go on a date tonight," he said abruptly.

"What?"

"You're right. You're human enough to need some time for us to get to know each other. Meet me at Wolf Kitchens at six and we'll go out to dinner when I get off shift."

"Was that an order or an invitation?" I snapped, still irritated by his refusal to stay with me.

"Both."

I sighed deeply. "Fine, I'll meet you tonight, but only if you take me to that Italian place downtown. I'm dying for some gnocchi."

"It's a date."

Two weeks later...

"How's it going with Charles?"

My sister Meri and I were having a drink at Murphy's Bar while we waited for Cami to get done with her shift at the store. The three of us were going to see the new Barbie movie as soon as she got off work.

"We're dating now."

Meri frowned. "You're dating your mate? I didn't know shifters could do that. They're not known for their patience."

"He wanted to mark me the first time we were together, but I was like, I need some time to sort through my feelings, you know? Being mated is a big decision. It's more final than getting married. So now we're just dating."

"Why do you look so glum about it?"

I leaned forward, mindful of all the shifters with enhanced hearing in the bar. "He won't sleep with me again until I agree we can be mates."

"Oh. Well. I guess it's nice to go slow sometimes."

I clutched her wrist. "You don't understand. Moving from the most incredible sex fest of my life to necking on the couch is torture, Meri. Pure torture. I'm so wound up all he has to do is glance in my direction and I'm ready to come."

Meri rolled her lips in, trying not to laugh. "Maybe you need to seduce him."

"You know what? I think you're right. And I know just when and how to do it," I responded as an idea began to form in my mind.

We both looked up as Cami joined us. "What's up, girls?"

"Charles won't give Pepper sex until she agrees to be officially mated, and Pepper is super horny so she's going to seduce him."

Cami started laughing. "Why don't you do a seduction spell?"

I sent her an annoyed look. "You know we're not supposed to do magic that overrides people's free will."

My sister shrugged. "It's more like nudging him along to what he already wants to do."

"Knowing me, I'd mess that up worse than you messed up the love potion that brought you Stephen. You know I don't have reliable magic."

I looked up as a couple approached our table. It was one of the Grey cousins and her new mate. I couldn't remember her name, but I'd gone to school with her older brother. The young woman was a waitress at the Italian restaurant where Charles and I ate dinner a couple of weeks ago. She'd been handing me my plate of gnocchi when we heard a growl through the window. Her mate was walking down the street, looked in the window, and the rest was history. Another new mate match in Greysden, courtesy of Pepper Rosewater.

"Pepper, I wanted to say thank you," the woman said warmly. "I'd always heard you helped people find their mate, so I was excited when you sat at one of my tables. I just didn't expect it to happen so fast."

She squeezed the other wolf's hand. "Brian and I are really grateful for you helping us find each other."

The male wolf nodded in agreement. "Thank you, Pepper."

"I'm just glad I could help," I said when they looked at me expectantly. "Congratulations to you both."

As they walked off in a cloud of happiness, Cami leaned forward eagerly.

"Pepper, it's magic!"

"What?"

She grabbed my hand. "Ever since Aunt Diane's spell started wearing off, you've been connecting people with their mates. Don't you see? You have a magical gift, you help people find love."

I looked at her skeptically, but Meri nodded vigorously. "Oh my goddess Pepper, it's true. You help fate along and bring people love and happiness when you least expect it. You're like a love witch."

"I don't think that's a thing," I said, although as the idea took root inside my heart it somehow felt right.

Thinking back, I realized that the mate finder thing had only started a few months before Jane came to town, wondering why she could suddenly do magic. And the stronger my magic got, the more matches I'd made. Cami was right, I did have some powers. All the time I'd been looking for something that was already inside me.

"A love witch, huh? I guess that's better than nothing."

Charles

Donald and I planned to do the soft opening for the restaurant on a Friday night so we'd have the weekend to recover. Openings were always nerve wracking, and while a soft opening generally had a friendlier audience, there was also that additional pressure of wanting to impress family and friends.

I'd invited the entire Rosewater family to the event and set them up at a large table in the corner. With the twins in highchairs at either side of the table, Sage and Edward sat on one side with Cami and Stephen, and Preston, Meri, and Pepper sat across from them. As I hustled around the restaurant, I could feel Pepper's eyes following me everywhere.

She seemed different tonight. Usually she dressed pretty casually, favoring jeans and leggings with tank tops and sweaters. But tonight, she was wearing a dark red wrap dress that clung to her curves, the tie at her waist the only thing holding the fabric together. She'd paired the dress with knee high black leather boots with a heel that added a good two inches to her height. Pepper was also wearing makeup for the first time since I'd met her. I took one look at those blood red lips, picturing them wrapped around my cock, and I'd nearly come in my pants.

It had been killing me not to sleep with her again, but she'd been right that day we'd talked in the hallway. She wasn't a shifter, and she needed more time to get used to the mating thing. So, we'd downshifted into dinners and watching movies, and we'd very carefully avoided moving past second base. Well, I'd been careful anyway; Pepper had tried repeatedly to round third. It had been torture.

Pepper sashayed up to me at the end of the dinner service, those beautiful eyes of hers sparkling with mischief. Something about her manner reminded me of a cat stalking her prey.

"Hey, great job tonight. Everything is delicious."

Pepper placed her palm on my chest, making my heart thump painfully underneath my white chef's jacket. I covered her hand with mine and stared into her eyes a little longer than was strictly appropriate for someone standing in the middle of a crowded dining room.

"Do you like my dress?" she asked silkily, waving her free hand down her body. My eyes followed the movement, noting the way the fabric highlighted her womanly curves.

I gulped audibly. "Yeah. It's real pretty."

She leaned closer and whispered, "Funny thing about this dress. All I have to do is tug this tie...," her fingers went to her belt, "and it just drops right off me. Oh, and in case you were wondering, I'm not wearing panties."

I looked around frantically for Donald. He was standing at a table with Janice and her parents but came right over when he saw the look on my face.

"Do you need to go, boss?" he asked with a knowing smile.

I nodded. All the blood had gone to my cock, leaving me unable to do anything else, like string together a sentence. Donald gave me a thumbs up.

"I'll take care of closing up. You kids have fun."

The words weren't even fully out of his mouth before I'd grabbed Pepper by the hand and pulled her out of the restaurant and into the parking lot. I practically shoved her into the passenger seat of my car and drove as quickly as I dared back to Rosewater Manor. The five-minute drive out of town had never seemed so long before. Neither of us said a word the entire time, but the air between us seemed to vibrate with anticipation.

Once we reached the house, I dragged her out of the passenger seat and tossed her over my shoulder, then I raced up the stairs to Pepper's suite.

"You're going to drop me," she laughed.

I clamped a hand over her ass to keep her in place.

"Are you feeling eager?" she teased as I slammed the door behind us and set her back on her feet.

"I know I said I'd give you time, Pepper, but I can't go another day without being inside you again."

I was a strong man, but no man was strong enough to resist a woman wearing that dress with no panties. Not when that woman was his fated mate.

"You're the one who forced celibacy on us," she reminded me.

Her fingers toyed with the belt at her waist. "I've been ready to go since the last time you left my bed."

Pepper winked. She turned on her heel and as she walked towards the bedroom, the dress slid off her shoulders, leaving her only in her bra and those sexy boots. I tore off my shirt then walked behind her, my eyes fixed on her delicious ass.

Pepper raised one eyebrow when she noticed my bare chest, and then she licked those red, red lips.

"Take off your pants," she ordered as she reached behind her and unclasped her bra. Her round breasts swayed as they were released, damned near hypnotizing me. "I want you, Charles. Now."

She didn't have to ask me twice. I kicked off my shoes and removed my pants and boxers in record time. Pepper's eyes widened as my thick cock bounced against my abdomen. It was already fully erect, pre-cum glimmering at the tip.

"Well, someone is happy to see me," she said coyly, reaching out to wrap her finger around my dick.

She gave me two or three firm jerks before I pulled away from her.

"You keep that up and I'm going to be finished before this is all over." My voice was so deep and rough I scarcely recognized it.

"So?"

She dropped to her knees and my heart seemed to stop beating. Leaning forward, she licked around my shaft like it was a lollipop before taking me into her mouth. I groaned as the tip of my penis hit the back of her throat. My animal was pressing against me, begging to come out to finally claim our mate, and I dug my claws into my palms trying to hold him back.

Pepper bobbed up and down on my dick, humming in pleasure as she watched me from beneath her eyelashes. It didn't take long before I was shooting my load down her throat. She drank down every drop, then licked her lips like she was looking for more.

I growled, the sound more animal than human, then picked her up under her arms and tossed her onto the bed. She was still bouncing when I shoved my shoulders between her thighs. Diving right in, I licked and teased the outer lips of her pussy until she was shaking with pleasure.

"Charles, please!"

I loved hearing her beg. Sliding my tongue inside her channel, I licked her up and down, gathering her cream on my tongue. Pepper was making whimpering noises when I finally focused my attention on her clitoris, circling it roughly and then sucking it into my mouth. It didn't take long before she came apart with a cry of pleasure, shaking beneath me.

But I wasn't done with her. I was already rock hard again, so I crawled up her body, stretching out on top of her. I balanced on my forearms and looked down into her eyes while I notched my cock against her opening.

"Tell me you want me, mate," I ordered.

"I want you."

I slid inside her slowly, making us both groan, not stopping until I bottomed out inside her and our hips met. Despite her earlier orgasm, her pussy was clamped tightly around me. Lowering my forehead to hers, I stared into her eyes.

"There's no going back now, Pepper, you understand that, right? This is forever."

She nodded.

"I need the words. Please, tell me that you'll be my mate."

I wanted her to say it. Needed her to say it. She paused long enough that I started to get nervous. Then she gave me a tiny smile that I knew I'd remember for the rest of my life.

"Do it, Charles. I want you to make me your mate."

Deep inside me, my animal howled in triumph. I kissed her roughly as my hips started pounding against hers, sinking deeper and deeper inside her until I wasn't sure where she started, and I ended.

Pepper wrapped her legs around my waist, lifting her hips to meet me as I dragged my pelvis against her clit with every stroke. It didn't take long until my mate was breaking apart again. She shuddered beneath me with her eyes screwed shut in pleasure, softly chanting my name like it was the only thing keeping her tethered to reality.

My mate squeezed me so hard it triggered my own orgasm, and as I found my release, I lowered my head and bit into her neck, binding us together for the rest of our lives. We both cried out in pleasure as the mate bond activated. A glow of magic surrounded us as one orgasm led to another, this one even better than the last one. Euphoria filled every part of my body and soul, leaving me feeling like a new man.

My arms collapsed and I dropped down on top of my mate, panting heavily. After a minute, Pepper tapped my shoulder, making me realize I was squishing her, so I rolled over and pulled her close to me, wrapping her in my arms.

"I love you, Pepper."

"That's just the orgasm talking," she teased sleepily. "Tell me again when we're not boneless."

"I'll tell you every single day for the rest of our lives," I promised.

Right before she fell asleep Pepper whispered, "I love you too, mate."

Epilogue – Pepper

Nine months later...

"Birth is a natural part of life. Embrace the pain, dear, let the life force flow over you."

My arm shot out and grabbed my mate's collar, bringing him down to eye level. Charles looked scared, and well he should be.

"I hate you right now," I hissed. "I hate you with every fiber of my being. Your humongous mutant child is clawing his way through my uterus while your mother is talking nonsense about life force."

Sparks flew from my fingers, making his shirt start to smoke.

"You have exactly thirty seconds to get her out of her and find out where the nurse is with my epidural before I kill you both. And I promise you, I will make you suffer."

Charles' eyes widened. When I released his collar, he jumped back out of arm's reach, patting the smoldering fabric of his shirt.

"Okay Mom, time to go wait in the waiting room with everyone else."

Ignoring his mother's protests, he dragged her out of the room. I wasn't even sure how she'd gotten in here. My own mother hadn't been allowed in. Given that I was pushing forty and it was my first child, the doctor had deemed me a 'geriatric pregnancy', which was a real hit to the ego.

Somehow my mate had managed to knock me up, despite my IUD, and I was almost positive it was the night we'd become mates. Charles was thrilled that he'd demonstrated his supposed virility by sneaking one past the IUD and while I'd always wanted a kid, I wished we could have had some more time together as a couple before it happened.

I rubbed my belly, mentally telling the little one they were wanted and loved, but I would have preferred that they waited a bit before making an appearance. The baby responded by poking me with his tiny little claws. I had no doubt the little guy was going to be a shifter of some sort. And definitely a boy.

A frazzled nurse walked in, pulling an IV stand behind her.

"That had better be an epidural or I swear to fuck I'm going to turn you into a toad."

Not that my magic had evolved that much, but what she didn't know wouldn't hurt her. The nurse rolled her eyes. Working in a town full of shifters and magical beings, she was likely used to strong personalities. But to her credit, she got to work administering the drug while my mate hovered nearby.

After we'd officially mated, Charles moved into my suite at Rosewater Manor and although we considered moving into our own place, we decided to stay put. We both loved living with my parents, and we'd been able to do a little remodeling to connect my suite with the one next door, making a larger space for our growing family.

Wolf Kitchens was going well, and the restaurant had become popular enough that people from neighboring towns were coming to Greysden to get a taste of the delicious menu. The first semester of culinary training already had a waiting list.

Everything was going great, other than the fact that I was tired of being pregnant and this damned baby seemed determined to kill me on his way out. Finally, the epidural started to take effect and I felt the sweet relief of the pain medication. An hour later Charles and I welcomed little Eva into the world.

"I thought for sure she was a boy," I said, staring at her scrunched up little face while she slept against my chest.

"Me too," Charles laughed. He looked a little dazed.

We'd told the doctor that we didn't want to know the sex of the baby, but somewhere along the line we'd both decided it was a boy. We hadn't even picked out a girl's name, but when the doctor told us we had a daughter, the name Eva was the first thing that popped out of my mouth. We both knew it fit our surprise daughter. She was going to be a badass, that's for sure.

Charles was in the bed next to me, his arm around my shoulders as he looked at little Eva like she was a miracle. And I guess she was. All new life was a miracle.

And so was love. I'd accepted that love was my magical gift, and over the last nine months I'd somehow helped facilitate twelve more couples finding true love. Several people had suggested that I give up my graphic design business and open a supernatural matchmaking agency instead.

"I love you so much, mate," Charles whispered.

His voice was rough, and I was pretty sure he'd been crying during the delivery, but I'd been a little too preoccupied with pushing out a baby to worry about him.

"I love you too," I said tiredly. "I suppose we should let the family in here to see the baby before your mother and my mother tear this place down."

He pressed his lips against my cheek. "In a minute, Pepper. Right now, let's just be alone as a family."

When our families came in later, they found the three of us cuddled in my hospital bed, fast asleep.

***

If you liked this book, please leave a review, and let me know! Want more of the Rosewater family and the magical world of Greysden? Check out all the books in this world at books2read.com/rl/Greysden[1].

Keep reading for a special except from "Wolf Doctor[2]", book one of the fan-favorite "Bite-Sized Shifters" paranormal romantic comedy series.

---

1. https://books2read.com/rl/Greysden

2.   **https://books2read.com/u/4AOXXK**

Special Preview

Wolf Doctor: A Paranormal Romantic Comedy

Twilight. Colt's favorite time of the day.

Stripping off his clothes, he took a deep breath, inhaling the scents in the air. He broke into a run and felt his body change mid-stride. In less than thirty seconds he had transformed from man to wolf.

Muscles and bone lengthening as gray hair sprouted all over his body, almost white in some places. His sharp canine teeth extended from his thickening jaw. He felt his tail grow behind him and he wagged it happily from side to side as he increased his pace, moving so fast his paws seemed to barely touch the ground.

Colt's senses were immediately heightened. His vision was sharper, his ears taking in even the softest sound, and his nose twitched with the wonderful scents of the pristine forest.

He headed through the woods, exhilarating in the feeling of free movement. His wolf loved to run. He hadn't shifted in almost a week. Too long. He needed this. He needed to shift and let his wolf run as much as he needed oxygen or food.

Speaking of food, he could use a snack. He scented a group of hares a mile away and headed in that direction at a gallop. His paws ate up the ground as he tracked the smaller beasts, stopping occasionally to sniff the ground and pick up their trail.

There, up ahead, he saw a flash of fur. He moved quickly, ears pinned back, as his wolf took over, the ultimate predator.

He could smell the fear on the hare as it took off, running for its life. Colt pulled his gums back in a canine smile. He loved the chase. The harder the capture, the better it tasted.

He sped up, following the hare instinctively as it took a sharp turn to the side. He pounced, leaping after the hare. Suddenly his feet hit air. And then he was falling. Fast.

Oh crap. He had overshot and gone right over the edge of the bluff. He could practically feel the stupid hare laughing at him as he tumbled down the embankment, scrambling but unable to stop his downward momentum.

He whined as his body hit the road below with a heavy thump.

Before he could recover he heard the squealing of brakes and suddenly he was airborne again. He landed on the asphalt a second time, feeling bones breaking and muscles tearing. He smelled the scent of his own blood and dimly heard voices as he struggled to stay conscious.

"Oh my god Dennis, you hit that poor dog!" The woman sounded upset.

"I'm not sure that it's a dog Sandy, it might be a wolf," someone, presumably Dennis, responded.

Not a dog, his wolf snipped in his head, clearly offended.

Really, that's your top worry right now? he asked his wolf.

Like all shifters, Colt shared space in his mind with his animal. He and his wolf shared not only the same body, but also the same consciousness.

He noted dimly that the humans who had hit him had exited their truck and were watching him cautiously from where they had stopped. He thought about getting up and whined again. The pain was terrible. It was impossible to move.

"He's bleeding and he's in pain," Sandy said, her voice sounding closer. "We have to get him to the animal hospital."

"There's no way he's going to survive," Dennis answered. "Let me get my shotgun out of the truck and I'll put the poor thing out of his misery."

Colt lifted his head in alarm, although it cost him dearly. He made eye contact with the woman, trying to communicate with her. He tried to make himself look sad and unthreatening. He did not want to die on the side of the road, and he definitely did not want to be put down by some random human with a shotgun. With his luck the guy would be a bad shot and make his injuries even worse.

"NO," Sandy said firmly. "You are not shooting him Dennis. Get the tarp. We'll put him in the back and drive him to the vet."

"He's a wounded animal Sandy," Dennis argued. "He may attack us, especially if he is a wolf."

Sandy continued to hold Colt's gaze. "No, he won't," she replied. "Come on, let's get him some help."

Colt passed out, not knowing who would win their argument. He just hoped it was Sandy.

He did not feel the couple cautiously wrapping him in a tarp and dragging him up into the back of their pick-up. He didn't feel himself sliding around in the truck bed as they raced to the animal hospital. He didn't hear the people loading him onto a gurney and wheeling his large body into the hospital. Both his body and his mind were completely shut down now, blissfully blocking the pain.

Then he felt it. A jolt of happiness and peace.

He opened his eyes, staring through the pain as an angel looked down at him. The overhead light glowed behind her like a halo. Thick brown hair framed her beautiful face. Her eyes were deep brown and impossibly kind.

"What happened?" his angel asked. Her voice made him feel calm. She seemed familiar.

"I think he took a header off a cliff. I think he came rolling down from up above. Suddenly there he was, falling onto the road right in front of us," Dennis explained. "Before I could stop, I hit him with my truck. I didn't do it on purpose, he seemed to come out of nowhere."

The angel's hand dropped gently to his head, rubbing him softly between his ears. He closed his eyes again, pressing against the warmth of her hand and whining softly. He had one thought before he passed out again. *Mate!*

***

For more of Colt and Valerie's story, check out "Wolf Doctor" by Rose Bak. Available now for download[1] at all major online retailers. Binge the whole series today.

---

1. *https://books2read.com/u/4AOXXK*

Other Books by Rose Bak

Magical Midlife Series
Beltane Magic (prequel)
Love Potion
Psychic Flashes
Halloween Surprise
Giant Love
Kitchen Magic
Alien Feeling
Bite-Sized Shifters Paranormal Romance Series
Long Distance Wolf
Wolf Doctor
Kat's Dog
Designer Wolf
Wolf Sheriff
Cocktail Wolf
Second Chance Wolf
Runaway Wolf
Holidays with the Shifters Series
Santa's Claws
Bear Humbug
Jingle Bear
Silver Paws
Joy to the Wolf
Lion's Heart
Boozy Book Club Series
Beach Reads
Bubbly & Billionaires
Martinis & Mysteries
Bourbon & Bikers
Midlife Madness

Extra Innings
The Proposal Solution
The Good with Numbers Holiday Romance Series
Love Unmasked
The Thanksgiving Scrooge
Maid for Christmas
Countdown to Love
Valentine's Lottery
Christmas Angel
Loving the Holidays Contemporary Romance Series
Dating Santa
New Year's Steve
Independence Dave
Comfort & Joy
Faking It with the Detective
Dropping the Ball
Island Getaway
Midlife Crisis Contemporary Romance Series
Summer Wedding
Roasting with Rob
Christmas Punch
Disaster Planning
Saving Texas
Texas Christmas
Factory Reset
Tempted at Midnight
Canadian Doctor
Second Chance to Score
Silver Fox Falls Midlife Romance
Unexpected Gift
Unexpected Love
Unexpected Life

The Oliver Boys Band Contemporary Romance Series
Until You Came Along
Rock Star Teacher
Rock Star Writer
Rock Star Neighbor
Rock Star Lawyer
The Diamond Bay Contemporary Romance Series
Brand New Penny
Fresh as a Daisy
Right as Rain
Reunited Series
Together Again
Finding My Baby
King of the Reunion
Caught by My Best Friend
Standalones
Beach Wedding
Jessie's Girl
Non-fiction
What to Do If You Find a Cougar in Your Living Room: Self-Care in an Uncaring World
It's All About Relationships: Reflections on Love, Friendship, and Connection

Catch up with these and other stories coming soon. Join my newsletter for more information[1] or follow my author page on your favorite retailer.

About the Author

Rose Bak has been obsessed with books since she got her first library card at age five. She is a passionate reader with an e-reader bursting with thousands of beloved books.

Although Rose enjoys writing both fiction and nonfiction, romance novels have always been her favorite guilty pleasure, both as a reader and an author. Rose's contemporary romance books focus on strong female characters over thirty-five and the alpha males who love them. Expect a lot of steam, a little bit of snark, and a guaranteed happily ever after.

Rose lives in the Pacific Northwest with her family, and special needs dogs. In addition to writing, she also teaches accessible yoga and loves music. Sadly, she has absolutely no musical talent, so she mostly sings in the shower.

Please sign up for the Rose Bak Romance newsletter[1] to get a free book and keep up to date on all the latest news. You can also follow Rose on Facebook[2], Instagram[3], Twitter[4], Goodreads[5], or Bookbub[6].

---

1.   https://storyoriginapp.com/giveaways/62ee758e-068f-11eb-904e-c373f6014fe1

2.   https://www.facebook.com/AuthorRoseBak

3.   https://www.instagram.com/authorrosebak/

4.   https://twitter.com/AuthorRoseBak

5.   https://www.goodreads.com/authorrosebak

6.   https://www.bookbub.com/authors/rose-bak

Don't miss out!

Visit the website below and you can sign up to receive emails whenever Rose Bak publishes a new book. There's no charge and no obligation.

https://books2read.com/r/B-A-VATM-PIYXC

Connecting independent readers to independent writers.

Milton Keynes UK
Ingram Content Group UK Ltd.
UKHW011138010424
440421UK00001B/92